Mrs Pepperpot in the Magic Wood

Alf Prøysen was born in Norway in 1914. He started writing when he was in his early twenties and wrote many successful children's books. He also produced radio programmes for children and wrote a weekly column in one of Norway's largest daily newspapers.

When his Mrs Pepperpot books first appeared they were an immediate success and have been loved by children all over the world ever since. Alf Prøysen died in 1971.

Once you have finished reading *Mrs Pepperpot in the Magic Wood* you may be interested in reading the Afterword by Lance Salway on page 90.

Also by Alf Prøysen

MRS PEPPERPOT TO THE RESCUE

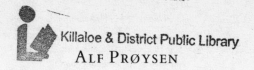
ALF PRØYSEN

Mrs Pepperpot in the Magic Wood and Other Stories

TRANSLATED BY MARIANNE HELWEG
ILLUSTRATED BY SIÂN BAILEY

PUFFIN BOOKS

PUFFIN BOOKS

Published by the Penguin Group
Penguin Books Ltd, 27 Wrights Lane, London W8 5TZ, England
Penguin Books USA Inc., 375 Hudson Street, New York, New York 10014, USA
Penguin Books Australia Ltd, Ringwood, Victoria, Australia
Penguin Books Canada Ltd, 10 Alcorn Avenue, Toronto, Ontario, Canada M4V 3B2
Penguin Books (NZ) Ltd, 182–190 Wairau Road, Auckland 10, New Zealand

Penguin Books Ltd, Registered Offices: Harmondsworth, Middlesex, England

This translation first published by Hutchinson Junior Books Ltd 1968
Published in Puffin Books 1972
Published in this edition 1995
5 7 9 10 8 6 4

Text copyright © Alf Prøysen, 1968
This translation copyright © Hutchinson Junior Books Ltd, 1968
Illustrations copyright © Siân Bailey, 1995
Afterword copyright © Lance Salway, 1995
All rights reserved

Typeset by Datix International Limited, Bungay, Suffolk
Printed in England by Clays Ltd, St Ives plc
Set in 12/15 pt Monophoto Bembo

Contents

Mrs Pepperpot
in the Magic Wood

Mrs Pepperpot, as you may remember, lives on a hillside in Norway. Behind her house there is an old fence with a gate in it. If you walk through that gate, says Mrs Pepperpot, you walk straight into the Magic Wood.

It's really just a little copse with larch and spruce and birch trees, but in spring the ground is covered with snowdrops – the whitest carpet you ever saw, and round a big mossy stone a patch of violets makes a bright splash of colour. The birch trees seem more silvery in here and the pale green branches of the larch trees more feathery as they sway over the stream that trickles down the hillside. And in and out of the long grass the weasel has made a pattern of little winding paths. It is very beautiful.

But Mrs Pepperpot likes it even better in winter when the Magic Wood has a thick carpet of snow and the icicles sparkle from the branches. Then all is silent except for the scrunch, scrunch of Mrs Pepperpot's boots as she walks through the snow.

It was a day before Christmas, and Mrs Pepperpot had asked her husband to cut her a small Christmas tree in the Magic Wood. But he was so busy at his work that he hadn't time to do it, so Mrs Pepperpot decided to take the axe and cut it down herself. As the snow was slippery, she took a stick with her. She soon reached the little fir-tree and, after marking a circle round it with her stick, she lifted the axe to start chopping.

Then the awful thing happened! You know, the thing that keeps happening to Mrs Pepperpot at the most inconvenient moments: she shrank to the size of a pepperpot.

'I'll have to find a small stick,' she said, 'it'll help me to plough a path through the snow. Ah well, I could be in a worse fix, I suppose, and I ought to be used to it by now.'

'Hi!' shouted a small voice quite close above her.

'What was that?' said Mrs Pepperpot, who had nearly jumped out of her skin, she was so surprised.

'It's me!' said the little voice. And now Mrs Pepperpot could see a tiny boy no bigger than herself, standing by her side.

'Well, come on; don't just stand there! They're all sitting inside, crying their hearts out because they think the ogre has eaten you. We must hurry home and surprise them.'

Without waiting for an answer, the little fellow bent down to a hole in the snow and started to crawl into it.

'Well,' thought Mrs Pepperpot, 'I may as well go and see what this is all about; he seems to know me, even if I don't know him.'

She left the axe and tucking the stick she had found under her arm she bravely crawled after the boy into the hole. It was quite a long tunnel which led to a little door. The boy knocked, but from behind the door there was such a noise of wailing and weeping that at first no one answered his knock. But when he had knocked again the bolt slid back and the door was opened by a young girl with a ladle in her hand. The room was brightly lit by a fire over which hung a steaming pot. Mrs Pepperpot, who was hidden behind the boy in the dark tunnel, could see three people inside and they were all looking most dejected as they went on with their crying.

The little boy stamped his foot. 'Stop that noise!' he shouted. 'Can't you see I've brought Betty Bodkin back?' and with that he took hold of Mrs Pepperpot's arm and dragged her into the middle of the room.

For a moment everyone stared at Mrs Pepperpot and then the wailing began afresh!

'Little Dick, what have you done? This isn't Betty Bodkin!' said the girl with the ladle.

Little Dick turned and had a good look at Mrs Pepperpot. Then he shook his fists at her and threw himself on the floor in what can only be described as a temper tantrum.

But Mrs Pepperpot had had enough of this nonsense: 'When you've all finished your catawauling,' she said, 'perhaps someone will tell me who you are and who I'm *supposed* to be. Then maybe I'll tell you who I *really* am.'

'It is a bit confusing,' said a fat little man who sat nearest the fire. 'We thought you were one of us, you see.'

'So I hear, but who are *you*?' Mrs Pepperpot was losing patience.

'Let me explain,' said the girl with the ladle, and as no one tried to stop her, she continued: 'You may not recognize us, but when you were little you knew us well enough. D'you remember your mother taking you on her lap sometimes to cut your nails? You probably didn't like it, and she would hold your hand and count your fingers one by one.'

'That's right,' said Mrs Pepperpot, 'and then she would sing me a little ditty that went like this:

> *Here is Thumbkin, fat and tubby,*
> *Here is Lickpot, always grubby,*

Longman next: he has his fiddle,
Now Betty Bodkin with her needle,
And little Dick who's just a tiddle.'

They all clapped their hands. 'There you are!' cried the girl, 'you haven't forgotten. And that's who we are – the finger people who live in the Magic Wood. This is Thumbkin,' she said, pointing to the fat little man by the fire.

'Pleased to meet you,' said Thumbkin, as Mrs Pepperpot shook hands with him.

'I used to find you a very comforting person,' said Mrs Pepperpot smiling.

'This is Longman, as you can see,' went on the girl, but the tall, thin fellow was so shy he held his fiddle behind his back and looked as if he'd like to vanish right away. 'I'm Lickpot. I do the cooking, you see,' said the girl.

Little Dick had now got over his disappointment. Taking another look at Mrs Pepperpot he said: 'You're so very like Betty Bodkin!'

'Just what happened to Betty Bodkin?' asked Mrs Pepperpot.

Immediately they all started talking at once: 'It was like this – we were out in the wood – we always wish the moon a Happy Christmas – it was such a glorious night!'

'One at a time, please!' said Mrs Pepperpot, holding her ears.

Lickpot raised her ladle to get order: 'Quiet now! I'll

5

explain. As they said, we went for a walk to greet the moon. Suddenly a huge ogre came along the path and we all had to rush into the tunnel to get out of his way. But Betty Bodkin tripped over her needle, and didn't manage it. The ogre picked her up in his great hand and put her in his pocket. Now we're all so worried about what has happened to her, and Christmas won't be Christmas without Betty Bodkin!'

'Perhaps the ogre has eaten her up!' said Little Dick, and he started to cry again.

'Oh, ogres aren't as bad as they once were!' said Mrs Pepperpot to comfort him. 'Besides, if she's as used to being small as I am, she'll know how to get out of tight corners.'

'If only we could find where the ogre lives, then perhaps we could rescue her,' said Lickpot.

'I'm sure we could, if we all pull together,' said Mrs Pepperpot. 'I think I have an idea where that ogre lives.'

'Will you show us the way?' asked Little Dick excitedly, and they all crowded round Mrs Pepperpot, tugging at her skirt.

'There's no time to lose,' she said and immediately started crawling back through the tunnel. The others followed, but when they got outside they found the road blocked by an enormous snowdrift.

'We'll never get through that!' said Thumbkin and looked quite ready to creep back inside to his warm fire.

It was quite a problem, and Mrs Pepperpot shut her

eyes so as to think better. Suddenly she remembered something very important; they were in the Magic Wood, where wishes come true if you wish hard enough. 'Quiet, everybody! I'm going to make a wish!' she said.

While they all stood very still she touched the snowdrift with her stick and said loudly: 'I wish this snowdrift to turn into a polar bear – a *friendly* polar bear – who can carry us all on his back and take us to the ogre's house.'

As soon as she finished speaking the snowdrift began to rise under them and they found themselves sitting on a soft, warm, white rug. Then the rug began to move forward, and Mrs Pepperpot could see two ears in front of her. She had ridden on a bear before, so she knew what bears like most – to be tickled between the ears. Gingerly she crawled towards the ears and perched herself between them.

'Do be careful!' warned Lickpot, who was clinging with all her might to the bear's fur. Longman was so frightened he was lying full length with his face buried, but Thumbkin and Little Dick were beginning to enjoy themselves, looking all around from their high seat.

When the bear felt his ears being tickled he purred – or rather, he rumbled – with contentment, and in no time at all he had carried Mrs Pepperpot and the finger people to the edge of the wood where there was a fence and a gate in it.

'Open the gate with your muzzle!' commanded Mrs

Pepperpot, and the big polar bear did just as she said and opened the gate.

Then they came to a house with a lighted window.

'Now I want you to lie down outside the door,' said Mrs Pepperpot, 'and you must wait there till I come out again – is that clear?'

The great creature just nodded his head slowly and settled down on the doorstep.

Mrs Pepperpot turned to the finger people: 'I'm pretty certain that I'll find the ogre inside this house,' she said.

'Don't you want us to help you rescue Betty Bodkin?' asked Little Dick, who was feeling quite chirpy now.

'No thanks, I think I can manage this by myself,' said Mrs Pepperpot. 'I just want you to wait here with Mr Polar Bear. If Betty Bodkin is there I'll bring her out to you, and then you can all go home.'

They all shook her hand warmly and wished her luck.

'Trust in me!' said Mrs Pepperpot, and swung her leg over the door-sill.

Just as she disappeared into the dark hall she grew to her normal size and walked into the dining-room.

There sat Mr Pepperpot; the tears were rolling down his cheeks and his sharp nose was quite red with crying. On the table by his side stood a small doll's bed Mrs Pepperpot had bought to give a little girl for Christmas, and in the bed lay Betty Bodkin, trying very hard to look like a doll! There were medicine bottles on the table as well, and a box of liquorice pills.

Mrs Pepperpot put her hands on her hips and said: 'Just what are you carrying on like this for?'

At the sound of her voice Mr Pepperpot looked up. He couldn't believe his eyes!

'Is that you? Is that really you, my own wife?' he cried, and caught hold of her skirt to see if she wasn't a ghost. 'I thought I'd lost you this time! I was going through the wood, searching for you, when I saw . . .' He stopped and stared at the little old woman in the doll's bed. 'But then, who's this? I picked her up in the snow and brought her home, thinking it was you who had shrunk again.'

'You silly man! Mixing me up with a doll that someone has dropped on the path!' said Mrs Pepperpot. Then, standing between him and the doll's bed, she carefully lifted Betty Bodkin up and wiped away the sticky medicine and liquorice pills her husband had tried to dose her with. Betty was just about to thank her, but Mrs Pepperpot made a sign for her to keep quiet and carried her towards the front door.

But Mr Pepperpot was so afraid his wife might vanish once more that he followed, holding on to her coat. As she leaned out of the door he asked: 'What are you putting the doll in that snowdrift for?'

'To get her back where she belongs,' said Mrs Pepperpot. 'Come and have your supper now.'

'Just a minute. I want to shovel that snowdrift away from the door-step first,' Mr Pepperpot said.

'Why? Are you afraid it'll walk in? Come on now, supper's ready.'

So Mr Pepperpot went into the kitchen to wash his hands and didn't hear his wife whisper to the snowdrift: 'Turn about, quick march and get them home as fast as you can!'

Later that night, when she was washing up, Mrs Pepperpot amused herself by singing the old ditty:

> *Here is Thumbkin, fat and tubby,*
> *Here is Lickpot, always grubby,*
> *Longman next: he has a fiddle,*
> *Now Betty Bodkin with her needle,*
> *And Little Dick who's just a tiddle.*

Mrs Pepperpot
and the Puppet Show

*I*t was a lovely summer's day, just the day for an
outing. The village sewing club had been invited to
a television show in the nearest town and they were
going by special coach.

Mrs Pepperpot was going too, and very excited she
was, as she had never watched a TV show in a theatre
before. Nor had any of the others, for that matter, and
they had all put on their best summer frocks and straw
hats with flowers.

On the way they prattled, as women do, and wondered what it would be like. They were going to see a puppet show, and Sarah South was sure that everyone else in the village would be envying them.

When they got to the town the bus stopped in the market square and they all got off. As they walked into the hall Norah North said: 'One thing we shouldn't do – smile at the camera – it looks so silly when you're watching TV.'

'Especially if you have gaps in your teeth,' said Mrs East, who could be a bit sharp when she liked.

They felt rather shy when they were given the front row of seats, but soon they were all comfortably seated with little bags of peppermints to munch. All except Mrs Pepperpot. Where was she?

Well, you know how she likes to poke her nose into things, and as they were walking along the passage to their seats, Mrs Pepperpot heard someone sniffing and crying in a little room next to the stage.

'That's funny!' she thought and peeped through the door. There she saw a full grown man with a top hat and long mustachios, sitting on a chair, crying like a baby.

'Well, I never!' said Mrs Pepperpot, but before she had time to follow the rest of her party, she SHRANK!

As she stood there, a tiny figure by the door in her bright summer dress and little straw hat, the puppet-man saw her at once. Quick as a knife he stretched out his hand and picked her up.

'*There* you are!' he said, holding her tightly between finger and thumb. 'I thought I'd lost you!'

Mrs Pepperpot was so terrified she didn't move, but when the man had had a closer look he said: 'But you're *not* my Sleeping Beauty puppet at all!'

'Of course I'm not!' said Mrs Pepperpot. The very idea!

'All the same,' said the puppet-man, 'as I can't find my most important puppet, you'll have to play her part. You'll look fine with a blonde wig and a crown and a veil, and I'll make your face up so that you'll be really beautiful.'

'You let me go this minute!' shouted Mrs Pepperpot, struggling to get out of the man's grip. 'Whoever heard of an old woman like me playing Sleeping Beauty?'

'Now, now! You have talent – you can act, I'm sure of it. And that's more than can be said of my other puppets who have to be handled with sticks and threads. You can walk and talk by yourself; you're just what I've always dreamed of and you'll bring me success and lots of money, you'll see.'

'Over my dead body!' said Mrs Pepperpot, who was still furious. 'I don't even remember the story of Sleeping Beauty.'

'I shall be telling the story,' explained the puppet-man, 'and you just have to do the things I say. But you don't come into the first act at all, so you can stand at the side and watch the other puppets through that crack in the curtain. Now it's time for the show to start, so be a sport and stay there, won't you?'

'I may and I mayn't,' said Mrs Pepperpot, so he lifted her gingerly down on the side of the puppet-stage which was set up in the middle of the real theatre stage.

Then the lights in the hall went out and those on the little stage went on. Mrs Pepperpot peeped through the hole in the curtain. The scene was a magnificent marble hall and she could see a puppet king and queen sitting on their thrones with their courtiers standing round. They were looking at a baby doll in a cradle.

The man began to speak behind the stage.

'There was once a king and a queen who had been blessed with a baby princess.'

'Lucky he didn't want me to lie in the cradle!' thought Mrs Pepperpot.

The man read on, telling how the good fairies were asked to the christening party and how they each gave the little princess a gift. Waving their wands over her cradle the fairies came in one by one.

'May you have the gift of Beauty!' said one.

'May you have the gift of Patience!' said another.

'I could certainly do with that gift,' said Mrs Pepperpot to herself. 'If there's anything I lack it's patience!'

When all the good fairies except one had waved their wands over the cradle, there was a terrible clap of thunder and the stage went completely dark for a moment.

'Goodness Gracious!' cried Mrs Pepperpot, 'I hope they haven't had a break-down!' She was beginning to get excited about the play now.

The lights came on again, and there was the bad fairy leaning over the baby with her wand.

'Ha, ha!' said the puppet-man in an old witch sort of voice. 'Today you are all happy, but this is *my* gift to the princess; in your fifteenth year may you prick your finger on a spindle and die!' And with that the bad fairy vanished in another clap of thunder and black-out.

'Well, if I'm the Sleeping Beauty, I'm a good deal more than fifteen years old and I'm still hale and hearty!' thought Mrs Pepperpot.

The puppet-man had now brought on another fairy to tell the king and queen that their daughter would not really die, but only go into a long, long sleep.

'One day a prince will come and wake her up,' said the fairy and that was the end of the first act.

The puppet-man was glad to see Mrs Pepperpot still standing there, but he didn't take any chances and caught her up roughly before she could protest. No matter how much she wriggled, she was dressed in the princess's blonde wig with a crown on top and a veil down her back. The worst part was when the puppet-man made up her face: Ough! It tasted like candle grease!

But when at last he put her down in front of a little mirror, she had to admit she looked rather wonderful.

'Now listen,' said the puppet-man. 'I don't mind if you make up your own speeches, but you must follow the story as I tell it, and one thing you must remember;

no advertising! It's strictly forbidden on this TV station.'

'Is it indeed!' said Mrs Pepperpot, who had not forgiven him for the rough treatment she had had – why, he'd even pulled her hair! 'We'll see about that!' she muttered.

But there was no time to argue, as the puppet-man was preparing to raise the curtain again. The scene was the same as before, but at first it was empty of puppets while the puppet-man read the introduction to the next part of the story.

'The king was so anxious to keep his only child safe from all harm, that he ordered every spindle in the country to be burned and forbade any more to be made. Meanwhile the princess grew up with all the gifts she had received from the fairies; she was good and beautiful, modest and patient, and everyone loved her. Then one day when she was fifteen years old the king and queen had gone out and she was all alone in the palace. She thought she would explore a bit.'

The puppet-man stopped reading and whispered to Mrs Pepperpot: 'This is where you come in! Walk across the marble hall and up the winding staircase in the corner. You'll find the witch at the top, spinning.'

He gave her a little push, and Mrs Pepperpot, in all her princess finery, walked on to the stage as grandly as she could. In the middle of the marble hall she stood still and looked for the staircase. When she saw it she turned to the audience and, pointing to the stairs, she said: 'I have to go up there; I hope it's safe! Always buy planks at Banks, the lumber man!' And up she went, holding her long skirt like a lady.

At the top of the stairs she found the witch puppet sitting, turning her spindle in her hand.

'Why, whatever are you doing with that old-fashioned thing?' asked Mrs Pepperpot.

'I am spinning,' said the puppet-man in his old witch voice.

'I call that silly,' said Mrs Pepperpot, 'when you can buy the best knitting wool in town at Lamb's Wool Shop!'

The audience laughed at this, but the puppet-man was not amused. However, he couldn't stop now, so he went on with the play, saying in his old witch voice: 'Would you like to spin, my child?'

'I don't mind if I do,' said Mrs Pepperpot. As she took the spindle from the witch's hand, the puppet-man whispered to her to pretend to prick herself.

'Ouch!' cried Mrs Pepperpot, sucking her finger and shaking it, 'I need a plaster from Mr Sands, the chemist!'

Again the audience laughed. The puppet-man now whispered to her to lie down on the bed to sleep. She asked if he wanted her to snore to make it more life-like.

'Of course not!' he said angrily. 'And I don't want any advertising for sleeping pills either!'

'Not necessary!' said Mrs Pepperpot, making herself comfortable on the bed. Then she raised her head for a moment and in a sing-song voice she spoke to the people in the audience.

> *The moment you recline*
> *On a mattress from Irvine*
> *You will fall into a sleep*
> *That is really quite divine!*

The puppet-man had difficulty in getting himself heard through the shouts of laughter that greeted this outrageous poem. But at last he was able to go on with the story how the princess slept for a hundred years and everyone in the palace slept too. When he got to the bit about the rose-hedge growing thicker and thicker round the walls of the palace, Mrs Pepperpot popped her head up again and said:

> *Quick-growing roses*
> *From Ratlin and Moses*

and then pretended to sleep again. She was really getting her revenge on the puppet-man, and she was enjoying every minute of it.

The puppet-man struggled on, but now the audience laughed at everything that was said, and he began to wonder if he should stop the show. He tried reading again: 'At length the king's son came to the narrow stairs in the tower. When he reached the top he opened the door of the little chamber, and there he saw the most beautiful sight he had ever seen – the Sleeping Beauty.'

While the gramophone played soft music to suit the

scene, the puppet prince walked up the stairs and came through the door. Mrs Pepperpot winked one eye at the audience and said:

> *I owe my beautiful skin*
> *To Complexion-Milk by Flyn.*

The puppet prince walked stiffly over to her bed and stiffly bent down and planted a wooden kiss on her cheek. But this was too much for Mrs Pepperpot: 'No, no!' she shrieked, jumping out of bed and knocking the prince flying, so that all his threads broke and he landed in an untidy heap at the bottom of the stairs.

Down the stairs came Mrs Pepperpot herself, and, jumping over the fallen prince, she rushed across the stage and out through the curtain, while the audience rolled in their seats and clapped and shouted for the princess to come back.

But once safely in the dressing-room, Mrs Pepperpot only just had time to snatch off her wig and veil and crown before she grew to her normal size. The little things she put in her handbag and she walked through the door as calmly as you please, only to be met by the poor puppet-man, who was wringing his hands and crying even worse than before the show.

'Whatever's the matter?' asked Mrs Pepperpot.

'My show's ruined!' he wailed. 'They'll never put it on TV again after all that advertising!'

'Advertising?' Mrs Pepperpot pretended to be surprised. 'Wasn't it all part of the play?'

But the puppet-man wasn't listening to her: 'Oh

dear, oh dear! What will become of me? And now I have no Sleeping Beauty at all!'

'You should treat your puppets with more respect,' said Mrs Pepperpot, 'they don't like being pushed about and having their hair pulled!'

With that she left him and walked out to the square to get on the bus. Her friends had all been too busy laughing and discussing the play to notice that she hadn't been with them. She sat down next to Sarah South who asked her if she had enjoyed the show.

'Oh, I had a lovely time! We all did, I mean!' said Mrs Pepperpot.

A few days later the puppet-man was mending the threads of his puppet-prince. He was feeling happier now, because all the newspapers had written that his way of playing Sleeping Beauty was new and original, and they all praised his performance very highly.

There was a knock on the door and the postman handed him a small parcel. He wondered what it could be, but when he opened it he stared with astonishment: inside was the princess's wig, crown and veil and also a reel of black thread and a little note.

The puppet-man read it aloud:

> *As back to you these things I send,*
> *May I be bold and recommend*
> *When next your puppet prince you mend,*
> *Try Jiffy's thread; it will not rend.*

Who had sent the parcel? And where did that little

puppet go who could walk and talk on its own?
'If only I knew!' sighed the puppet-man.

Midsummer Eve
with the Ogres

*I*n Norway everybody celebrates Midsummer Eve
with bonfires and fireworks and all sorts of fun. It is
so far north that the sun hardly goes down at all in
June, and on Midsummer Eve even the children stay
up all night, dancing and singing with the grown-ups.

Now, although Gapy Gob is a big ogre, he is very
much like a little boy as far as parties go; he just loves
them, and Katie Cook and Charlie Chop, his two little
human servants, take a lot of trouble to make every-

thing nice for him on Midsummer Eve.

This year they hadn't invited any guests: 'Let's just be ourselves,' said Gapy Gob, 'we can have fun together and there'll be more to eat!' The ogre does like his food.

They all worked hard to get ready for the night; even Gapy Gob decided to do his annual clean-out of the cow-shed while their only cow was grazing on the high mountain pasture. Katie was busy cooking in the kitchen; she made Gapy's favourite pudding with cream and best wheat flour and nuts and raisins floating in it. When it was cooked she sprinkled grated lemon rind over the top and put it in the larder. She had baked a special cake with malt beer in it and something else which she and Charlie kept secret from Gapy Gob – it was to be a surprise for him. There was also a big bowl of freshly picked strawberries from their own garden and thick cream to go with it.

Meanwhile Charlie was cutting green branches in the wood and brought them home to decorate the outside of their little house. He built a most imposing porch over the front door and put green leaves all round the windows. When Katie had finished cooking she went out to pick flowers and made pretty garlands to hang on the doors; one for the front door, one for the cow-shed door and even one for the larder, which was built on stilts behind the house. The whole place looked really beautiful when they had done, and they looked forward to showing Gapy Gob when he came home from milking the cow.

'We deserve a nice cool drink after all that!' said Katie, and went to the larder to fetch some fruit juice. But a moment later she called out to Charlie: 'Come quick! Someone's been in the larder and stolen the food!'

Charlie rushed round and, sure enough, not only the cream pudding and the malt cake had gone, but also a big tall candle that Charlie had made himself for Mid-summer Eve.

'But how could anyone get in?' he asked. 'You always carry the key in your belt, Katie.'

'I have the key, all right,' said Katie, 'but I must just have forgotten to lock the door when I went out to pick flowers.'

'Whatever will Gapy say?' Charlie wondered.

'We won't tell him yet. By this evening I'll think up something else we can have and there's still the strawberries and cream.'

So, when the ogre came home with the milk, they said nothing about what had happened.

Gapy admired all their decorations and then he rubbed his hands, saying: 'Oh boy, oh boy, oh boy! Am I looking forward to tonight!' And all the poor children could do was to smile and nod their heads.

Not long after, who should they see come tripping up the path but the ogress, Wily Winnie, and her cat, Ribby Ratsoup.

'What do they want?' said Gapy Gob, and the happy look disappeared from his face. Wily Winnie was very ugly and stupid, but she fancied Gapy Gob as a husband

and was always getting her cunning cat to think up ways of getting Gapy to visit her.

'Up to no good, I'll be bound!' said Charlie darkly.

But Wily Winnie was all smiles when she came up to them and wished them a polite 'Good Afternoon.' Ribby stood behind her, smirking and twirling her whiskers.

'It's so long since we saw you, Gapy Gob,' began the ogress, 'I thought it would be nice if you could come to my house tonight to celebrate Midsummer Eve.'

'Well, thanks, Wily Winnie,' said Gapy. 'It's kind of you to ask me, but –'

Katie chipped in and finished his sentence for him: 'We're having our own party here tonight, so he can't come.'

'No, I couldn't leave the children – not tonight!' said Gapy.

'But of course we want them to come too, don't we, Ribby?' cried Wily Winnie, but while she spoke she managed to put her heavy shoe on poor Katie's bare foot. Katie bit her lip; she wasn't going to cry.

'And we love little boys at our parties!' said Ribby, secretly digging her claws into Charlie's leg. He just shut his eyes and said nothing.

'Right oh!' said Wily Winnie. 'Then that's agreed – you'll all come tonight at seven o'clock and we shall have a lovely meal!'

As Gapy Gob couldn't think of any other good reason to say no, he thanked the ogress and she and

Ribby Ratsoup danced off down the path again. But as the afternoon wore on, the ogre and the children felt more and more gloomy at the thought of leaving their nice house in the sunshine to go tramping over the other side of the mountain where it was dark and dreary.

'She'll probably give us one of those horrible soups Ribby makes,' said Gapy, 'with rats' tails in it.'

'Better have the soup than no meal at all!' said Charlie, but Katie nudged him with her elbow and said loudly: 'Come along, we might as well go now,' and they set off for the ogress's house.

Wily Winnie and her cat had been decorating too. Ribby had dragged some fallen fir branches in from the wood because she couldn't use a saw or an axe with her paws. She had scattered them on the path outside the house while her mistress nailed up a crazy arrangement of sticks over the door which she fondly imagined looked very artistic.

Inside Ribby had swept the floor for once, but a heap of fishbones and other rubbish had been left in one corner, and it didn't smell very nice.

Wily Winnie was on the doorstep to greet Gapy. She said: 'I hope your servants won't mind giving Ribby a hand; I see Charlie has brought his axe, so perhaps he could cut us some wood for the cooking stove, and maybe Katie could lay the table, eh?'

'No,' said Katie, 'I couldn't. I'm a guest.'

'Oh, come on, Katie,' said Charlie. 'I don't mind cutting up a few logs, so you can give a hand too.'

Then he added in a whisper: 'It'll give us a chance to see what's cooking!'

So the children went out in the kitchen with Ribby, while in the front room Gapy sat down in one rocking chair and Wily Winnie in the other.

'I don't know what you see in those stupid children,' she began.

'They're not stupid,' said Gapy Gob. 'Katie's a wonderful cook, and we always have plenty of wood for the stove with Charlie around.'

'Well, *I* have a proposition to make,' said Wily Winnie.

'A proposition? What's that?' said Gapy, who didn't like long words.

'Let me put it this way!' said the ogress. 'What would you say if you could have just as good food as Katie's and all the wood brought in to keep you warm? Would you need the children then?'

Gapy looked confused: 'But I haven't anyone else to do those things!'

Wily Winnie gave his hand a playful slap: 'You silly!' she said. 'I'm talking about *us*! I mean, if I could give you lovely meals here and keep you warm as well, would you send Katie and Charlie packing – *would* you?' And she put her head on one side and smiled in what she hoped was a winning way.

But Gapy Gob just looked away and didn't answer, because he knew she was trying to catch him again.

'How aggravating you are!' cried the ogress. 'It's very rude not to agree to what a lady proposes, and I

27

would look after you like my own pet lamb, so I would!'

'I'm not a pet lamb!' muttered Gapy, but not too loudly, for he was very scared of Wily Winnie.

'Will you agree,' she went on, 'to send the children away after tonight if you like the food I give you? Say yes or no!'

Miserably Gapy nodded his head, more to stop the argument than anything. All he hoped now was that the food would be bad, so that he wouldn't have to part with Katie and Charlie.

At last the meal seemed to be ready. First Charlie brought in a tall candle and set it in the middle of the table and lit it. Then Ribby carried in the first course, which was a malt cake with a curious hump in the middle.

'D'you always bake your malt cake with a hump?' asked Katie, as they sat down to eat.

'A hump?' said Wily Winnie, noticing it for the first time. 'Oh yes, of course I do. Malt cake should have a hump.' She cut them all slices, and Gapy Gob had to admit that it was delicious. But the next moment he spat out a big mouthful; 'I bit on something hard!' he said, and there, right in the middle of the plate, was a tiny horse carved in wood.

'How very odd!' said Charlie Chop. 'That's just like the little horse I carved and put in *our* malt cake when Katie was baking it. I meant it to be a surprise present for Gapy.'

'My Ribby's very good at carving too,' said the

ogress hurriedly, 'and she put a horse in our cake, didn't you, Ribby?'

'That's right,' said the cat, 'whittled it with my own fair paw,' and she held up her right paw that had never done an honest stroke of work in its life. The children gave her such a look that she thought it best to go and fetch the next course in. When she came back with a large bowl of cream pudding, Gapy Gob just stared: 'How did you know that was my favourite pudding?' he asked.

'Ah!' said the ogress. 'A little bird told me that!'

'Flew over here, bowl and all, I suppose!' muttered Charlie, but Gapy was so busy scooping pudding into his mouth he didn't hear.

'It's just like ours at home,' he said between mouthfuls, 'and it has all the right things in it!'

'Oh yes,' said Wily Winnie, 'I always put nuts and raisins in!'

'I don't mean them,' said Gapy Gob, 'I mean the *secret* flavour; it was very clever of you to put that in.'

Wily Winnie couldn't think what that could be, so she turned to Katie and asked if she had put something in the pudding before it was brought in.

'Not in your kitchen!' said Katie.

'Well, never mind,' said the ogress, who seemed to be getting nervous: 'I think everyone's had enough. You may clear, Ribby!'

'What's the hurry?' asked Gapy, who was scraping his plate. 'At home Katie lets me have lots and lots of my favourite pudding.'

'You'll get too fat!' said Wily Winnie, as Ribby whisked the bowl away from the table.

'Look who's talking!' whispered Katie to Charlie, for the ogress was just about as wide as she was high.

'What's next?' asked Gapy Gob.

'That's all!' said Wily Winnie. 'Enough's as good as a feast, you know. Now we can all sit and watch the pretty candle burn while we play some guessing games.'

But Gapy was still hungry: 'We always have strawberries and cream at home on Midsummer Eve!' he said.

'We couldn't carry – I mean we don't *grow* strawberries on this side of the mountain,' said Wily Winnie. 'Come on now, what shall we play?'

'Let's guess what's inside the candle,' suggested Charlie.

'That's easy!' said the ogress, 'candles are made of tallow, of course!'

'It has a wick down the middle!' said Ribby.

'Clever Puss!' cried Wily Winnie, clapping her hands.

'Well, *I* guess there's something made of silver half-way down!' said Charlie Chop.

'Nonsense, boy, how could there be anything inside?' said Gapy.

'Wait and see!' said Charlie, so they all watched the candle burn, and when it came to the middle it sputtered and out fell a little silver ring on to the table.

'Well, I never!' said Gapy. 'How did you know?'

'Because I put it there!' said Charlie. 'It was my

surprise present for Katie. And now we know who stole my candle!'

'And the malt cake I made and the cream pudding!' chimed in Katie.

'I don't know what you're talking about!' said the ogress.

'Nor do I,' said Gapy. 'Who stole what?'

'We didn't want to spoil your evening, Gapy,' explained Katie, 'but our party food was stolen from the larder today when I was out picking flowers and Charlie was building the porch.'

'I *see*,' said Gapy looking hard at Wily Winnie, who had backed away into a corner. 'So *that's* why the cream pudding tasted so good! It was Katie's all the time.' He was so angry that he pushed the table over and all the plates and dishes fell on the floor.

'Please don't be cross, Gapy!' pleaded the ogress, while her cat hid behind her. 'It was only a joke! Ribby and I wanted to have a little fun on Midsummer Eve, that's all!'

But Gapy Gob didn't even look at her. Taking Katie by one hand and Charlie by the other he led them out of the door. 'We'll go home now, children,' he said.

As they walked back over the mountain, they could hear the ogress throwing pots and pans at Ribby and shouting at the top of her voice: 'You stupid cat! It's all your fault; you and your crazy ideas! Get out this instant and bring me back enough wood to make a bonfire to roast you on!' and she chased the cat out of the door with a stick. Ribby ran as she had never run before, and she hid in the wood for three whole days and nights till her mistress had had time to cool her temper.

As for Gapy Gob and the children, they had a lovely feast of strawberries and cream when they got home. They sat under Charlie's green porch all night long, singing songs and telling stories. And they didn't even need the candle, because it never got really dark at all.

Mrs Pepperpot
and the Baby Crow

One summer's day when Mrs Pepperpot was
coming home from picking blue-berries in the
forest, she suddenly heard something stir in the heather.

'Oh dear,' she thought, 'I hope it isn't a snake.'

She picked up a strong stick and walked as softly as
she could towards the noise.

But it wasn't a snake; it was a baby crow which
must have fallen out of its nest. It was flapping its
wings and trying so hard to get off the ground.

'Poor wee thing!' said Mrs Pepperpot. 'What shall we do with you?'

Very gently she lifted it up and then she could see it had hurt one of its wings. So she put it into her apron pocket and took it home with her. When she got indoors she found a little doll's bed which she lined with soft flannel, and then she carried the baby crow up to the attic, so that Mr Pepperpot wouldn't know about it. He always got so cross when she brought creatures in.

Whenever her husband was out Mrs Pepperpot would sneak up to the attic with little titbits for the bird and watch it hop around on the floor. When it got stronger it could jump from one beam to the other, and soon the day came when it could really fly.

But by now Mrs Pepperpot had got so fond of the untidy ball of black fluff that she hadn't the heart to let it go. The days went by till one Monday morning Mrs Pepperpot woke up and said to herself: 'Today's the day. I'll have to let the bird out today.'

But then the weather turned nasty and she thought it would be better to wait till the next day.

On Tuesday morning the sun shone. In fact, it was very hot.

'Oh dear,' said Mrs Pepperpot, 'I'm sure there'll be a thunderstorm. The poor little thing would be frightened to death. We'd better wait till tomorrow.'

On Wednesday Mrs Pepperpot couldn't find the cat, and she was afraid it might be lurking somewhere outside the house, waiting to pounce on the baby crow. So she decided to wait till Thursday.

On Thursday she found the cat and shut it in the shed. The little crow was flying from beam to beam and quite clearly wanted to get out. When Mrs Pepperpot came up to the attic it flew on to her shoulder and pulled her hair with its beak, as much as to say: 'Come on, open that window!'

But Mrs Pepperpot had thought up another excuse. 'You see, my pet,' she said, stroking the little crow's back, 'when people have been ill, they have to rest a bit – they call it convalescing – before they can go out. I think you need a little more convalescing.'

'Caw, caw!' said the crow and flew off into a corner of the attic where it sulked the rest of the day.

On Friday Mrs Pepperpot spent a lot of time in the attic. She found all sorts of things to do up there, sorting out her boxes of old clothes and quite unnecessarily dusting the shelves. In between she sighed and she sniffed, and by the time her husband came home she was so out of sorts she had forgotten to cook him any supper.

'What's the idea?' said Mr Pepperpot. 'Can't a man even have a meal when he comes back from a hard day's work?'

'Eating! That's all you think of!' snapped Mrs Pepperpot. 'You can come back in half an hour.' And she turned her back on him and made a great noise with the saucepans so that he wouldn't notice she was crying.

'Well!' said Mr Pepperpot, 'I don't know what's the matter with you, but you seem to have lost the *rest* of your wits,' and with that he hurried out of the door, in case his wife should throw a plate after him.

But Mrs Pepperpot was too upset to throw plates; she just stood by the kitchen stove and cried because she couldn't bear to let the little crow fly.

When she went to bed she was feeling more sensible and she told herself she would do it for sure tomorrow. But then she remembered it was Saturday: 'So many people go out shooting on Saturdays, they might shoot my baby by mistake, or think it was lame and "put it out of its misery", as they say.'

So next day she went to the attic, and when the little crow flew over to her, she took it gently in her hand and talked to it soothingly. 'You must be patient a little longer. Today you might get shot, and tomorrow is Sunday and then there are so many trippers about you might get caught and put in a cage. You wouldn't like that, would you, my pet? No, let's wait till the beginning of the week when all is quiet again.'

The bird seemed to understand what she was saying, because it jumped straight out of her hand and flew up and pecked her nose!

'Temper, temper!' said Mrs Pepperpot and she didn't go near the attic the rest of the day.

On the Sunday she only had time to take some food and water up to the bird in the morning, as she was expecting visitors and, besides, Mr Pepperpot was home all day.

On Monday morning she had some nice bacon-rind which she took up as a special treat.

'Here we are, my little duck, something really nice for you!' she said.

But the little crow just glared at her from the highest beam and wouldn't come down.

There was a bee buzzing round the window, so, as Mrs Pepperpot was afraid it might sting her precious bird, she opened the window and let it out.

At that very moment she SHRANK!

'Caw, caw! At last!' squawked the little crow, and before she had time to get on her feet, Mrs Pepperpot felt herself being lifted into the air by her skirt, and away went the little crow with her out of the window!

As they flew over the roof and the trees they were joined by a whole crowd of big crows, all squawking together.

'Caw, caw! Welcome back!' they squawked.

One big crow flew up beside the young crow. In a deep throaty voice it said: 'Well done, young 'un. Bring her before the council! We'll all be there. Caw, caw!'

'Oh no!' cried Mrs Pepperpot, 'not that again!' Because she remembered the time she had had to sing at the Crow's Festival and they stole all her clothes!

But there was nothing she could do, dangling helplessly, as she was, in the little crow's beak.

All the crows were heading in the same direction and soon they swooped down and landed in a clearing in the forest. The little crow put Mrs Pepperpot down right in the centre, and all the crows stood in a big ring round her. She was very frightened indeed.

The big crow spoke first: 'You may begin, young 'un. Tell us what happened.'

So the little crow told them how Mrs Pepperpot had found it after it had fallen out of the nest, and how she had taken it home.

'Were you frightened?' asked the big crow.

'I suppose I was just as frightened as she is now,' said the little crow, looking at Mrs Pepperpot, who was shaking all over.

'What did the monster do to you?' asked another crow.

'I'm not a monster!' cried Mrs Pepperpot. 'I didn't do anything bad! I just kept him in a nice warm attic till he could fly.'

'That's right,' said the little crow. 'She took pity on me because I had hurt my wing.'

'But after the wing got better,' asked the big crow, 'did she still keep you shut up in the attic against your will?'

'She did,' said the little crow.

'It's a black lie!' shouted Mrs Pepperpot. 'You know I was going to let you out, but I had to be sure you would be safe. The first day you could fly it was raining cats and dogs.'

The big crow looked up at the sky: 'Hm, it looks as if it's going to pour any minute now. We'd better keep the little thing here till tomorrow, or she might get drowned walking home.'

'I'm not a "thing",' said Mrs Pepperpot.

'You called me a "duck",' said the little crow.

'But I *must* get home today,' said Mrs Pepperpot. 'I have to put the peas to soak for our pea-soup tomorrow.'

'And we can't let her go tomorrow, either,' went on the big crow, 'because that's the day we have a visit from Master Fox, and he might take her for a weasel.'

'Stuff and nonsense!' said Mrs Pepperpot.

'That's what I thought,' said the little crow, 'when you told me about the cat.'

'Perhaps we could let her go on Wednesday,' chipped in another crow.

'Wednesday!' cried Mrs Pepperpot. 'I must certainly be there then, because that's the day the fishmonger calls, and I've ordered two pounds of herring from him,' said Mrs Pepperpot.

The big crow shook its head: 'I'm afraid that fishmonger's van is too dangerous. It might run her down. She can go on Thursday.'

'Thursday! I *must* be home then; we get the big saw back from the grinder's that day, and I have to help my husband saw up logs.'

'Tut, tut! A little thing like you can't be allowed to saw logs!' said the big crow. He turned to the others: 'Don't you think it would be safer to keep her till Friday?'

'Yes, yes! Caw, caw!' squawked all the crows.

'Friday is my big cleaning day,' said Mrs Pepperpot, 'and if you don't let me go till then I shall have to do all my washing as well. It's not fair!' and she stamped her foot and shook her fists at the birds.

'Now, now,' said the big crow, 'temper, temper! Friday is an unlucky day, everyone says so. Saturday would be better.'

But this was too much for Mrs Pepperpot. She just sat down and buried her head in her apron and sobbed and sobbed. She thought she'd never get home!

'I only did it to be kind!' she hiccoughed. 'I was so very fond of the little crow!'

Just then she felt herself grow to her usual size, and when she looked round all the crows had scattered and were whirling overhead in the trees, cawing loudly.

Mrs Pepperpot wiped her eyes and straightened her hair. Then she started to walk home. As she walked she thought about the things the crows had said to her.

'I think maybe they're right. It isn't much fun to be in prison like that, day after day.'

But wait till you hear the strangest thing: since that day, whenever Mrs Pepperpot goes up to the attic and opens the window, that little crow comes flying in to sit on her shoulder! It never pecks her nose or pulls her hair, and Mrs Pepperpot always has a titbit for it in her apron pocket.

Mrs Pepperpot
Learns to Swim

*A*s you know, Mrs Pepperpot can do almost anything, but for a long time there was one thing she couldn't do: she couldn't swim! Now I'll tell you how she learned.

In the warm weather Mrs Pepperpot always took a short cut through the wood when she went shopping. In the middle of the wood is quite a large pool which the village children use. Here they play and splash about in the water. The older ones, who can swim, dive from a rock and race each other up and down the pool. They teach the younger ones to swim too, as there's no grown-up to show them. Luckily, the pool is only deep round the big rock and those who can't swim stay where it's shallow. But they're all very keen to learn, so they practise swimming-strokes lying on their tummies over a tree-stump and counting one-two-three-four as they stretch and bend their arms and legs.

Mrs Pepperpot always stopped to watch them, and then she would sigh to herself and think: 'If only I could do that!' Because nobody had taught *her* to swim when she was a little girl.

Some of the big boys could do the crawl, and the little ones tried to copy them, churning up the water with their feet and their arms going like windmills while everyone choked and spluttered.

'I bet I could learn that too!' thought Mrs Pepperpot. 'But where could I practise?'

One day when she got home, she decided to try some swimming-strokes in the kitchen, but no sooner had she got herself balanced on her tummy over the kitchen stool, when her neighbour knocked on the door asking to borrow a cup of flour. Another time she tried, she flung out her arms and knocked the saucepan of soup off the stove, and her husband had to have bread and dripping for supper. He was *not* pleased.

Every night she would dream about swimming. One night she had a lovely dream in which she could do the breast-stroke most beautifully. As she dreamed, she stretched forward her arms, bent her knees and then – Wham! One foot almost kicked a hole in the wall, the other knocked Mr Pepperpot out of bed!

Mr Pepperpot sat up. 'What's the matter with you?' he muttered. 'Having a nightmare, or something?'

'Oh no,' answered Mrs Pepperpot, who was still half in a dream. 'I'm swimming, and it's the most wonderful feeling!'

'Well, it's not wonderful for me, I can tell you!' said Mr Pepperpot crossly. 'You stop dreaming and let me have some peace and quiet.' And he climbed into bed and went to sleep again.

But Mrs Pepperpot couldn't stop dreaming about swimming. Another night she dreamed she was doing the crawl – not like the little ones, all splash and noise, but beautiful strong, steady strokes like the big boys, and one arm went up and swept the flower-pots from the window-sill and the other landed smack on Mr Pepperpot's nose.

This was too much for Mr Pepperpot. He sat up in bed and shook Mrs Pepperpot awake.

'You stop that, d'you hear!' he shouted.

'I was only doing the crawl,' said Mrs Pepperpot in a far-away voice.

'I don't care if you were doing a high dive or a somersault!' Mr Pepperpot was very angry now. 'All I know is you need water for swimming and not a bed. If you want to swim go jump in a swimming pool and get yourself a swimming teacher!'

'That's too expensive,' said Mrs Pepperpot, who was

now awake. 'I watch the children in the pool in the wood. One of these days, when they're all gone home, I'll have a try myself.'

'Catch your death of cold, no doubt,' muttered Mr Pepperpot and dozed off again. But a little while later there was a terrible crash, and this time Mr Pepperpot nearly jumped out of his skin.

There was Mrs Pepperpot, on the floor, rubbing a large lump on her forehead. She had been trying to dive off the side of the bed!

'You're the silliest woman I ever knew!' said Mr Pepperpot. 'And I've had enough! I'm going to sleep on the kitchen floor.'

With that he gathered up the eiderdown and a pillow, went into the kitchen and slammed the door.

Mrs Pepperpot was a bit puzzled. 'I can't have done it right!' But then she decided enough was enough and, wrapping herself in the only blanket that was left on the bed, she slept the rest of the night without any more swimming-dreams.

Then came a bright warm day when all the village children were going on a picnic up in the mountains.

'That's good,' thought Mrs Pepperpot, 'there'll be no one in the pool today and I can get my chance to have a try.'

So when she'd cleaned the house and fed the cat and the dog, she walked through the wood to the pool.

It certainly looked inviting, with the sun shining down through the leaves and making pretty patterns on the still water. There was no one else about.

She sat down on the soft grass and took off her shoes and stockings. She had brought a towel with her, but she'd never owned a bathing suit, and it didn't even occur to her to take her skirt and blouse off. Peering over the edge, she could see the water wasn't very deep just there, so she stood up and said to herself: 'All right, Mrs P., here goes!' and she jumped in!

But she might have known it — at this moment she SHRANK!

Down, down she went, and now, of course, the pool seemed like an ocean to the tiny Mrs Pepperpot.

'Help, help!' she cried, 'I'm drowning!'

'Hold on!' said a deep throaty voice from below. 'Rescue on the way!' And a large frog swam smoothly towards her.

'Get on my back,' he said.

Mrs Pepperpot was thrashing about with both arms and legs and getting tangled up in her skirt as well, but she managed to scramble on to the frog's knobbly back.

'Thanks!' she panted, as they came to the top, and she spat out a lot of water.

The frog swam quickly to the rock, which now seemed quite a mountain to Mrs Pepperpot, but she found a foothold all right and sat down to get her breath, while the frog hopped up beside her.

'You're certainly a good swimmer,' said Mrs Pepperpot.

The frog puffed himself up importantly: 'I'm the champion swimming teacher in this pool,' he said.

'D'you think you could teach me to swim?' asked Mrs Pepperpot.

'Of course. We'll begin right away, if you like.'

'The children do the breast-stroke first, I've noticed,' said Mrs Pepperpot.

'That's right, and frogs are very good at that. You climb on my back and watch what I do,' said the frog, as he jumped in.

It was a bit difficult to get off the rock on to the frog's back, but he trod water skilfully and kept as steady as he could. Soon she was safely perched and watched how the frog moved his arms and legs in rhythm. After a while he found her a little piece of floating wood and told her to hang on to that while she pushed herself along with her legs.

She got on fine with this till she suddenly lost her grip on the piece of wood and found herself swimming along on her own.

'Yippee!' she shouted with excitement, but the frog, who had been swimming close to her all the time, now came up below her and lifted her on to his back.

'That's enough for the moment,' he said, and took her back to the rock for a rest. 'You've got the idea very well, for a beginner.'

Mrs Pepperpot was feeling so pleased with herself, she wanted to go straight on and learn the crawl and swim on her back and everything, but the frog said: 'Not so fast, my dear; you've learned to keep afloat now, but you must go on practising the breast-stroke before you can do the other things.' But when he saw she looked disappointed, he said: 'I'll get my tadpoles to give you a show of water acrobatics, how's that? You get in and swim along with me to the shallow end; that's where they have their water circus.'

So they set off together, the frog making elegant circles round Mrs Pepperpot as she made her way slowly across the pool, trying to remember to keep her arms together and her legs from kicking in all directions. At last they got to the shallow part where there were reeds growing on the sandy bottom, and in and out of these hundreds of tadpoles were darting. There were all sizes from the tiniest things no bigger than a lady-bird to big ones with their front legs showing and some even had their back legs as well and were just about to shed their tails.

The frog found a small flat rock for Mrs Pepperpot to sit on and then he called all the tadpoles round him: 'Come on, children,' he croaked, 'I want you to show this lady all your best tricks. Let's see what you can do and remember what I've taught you.'

All the tadpoles immediately got into line, the biggest at the front, the smallest at the back, so that they looked like a long, winding snake. Talk of follow-my-leader! Whatever the front tadpole did, the others copied so exactly you would think they had all been tied together with string. First they swam to the top of the water, then they dived to the bottom, then they wove in and out of the reeds in a beautiful pattern. Then, like aeroplanes doing aerobatics, they rolled over and over and looped the loop and they even swam backwards, still keeping as smartly in line as any regiment of soldiers.

Mrs Pepperpot was very impressed, and the frog had puffed himself up so much, he was nearly bursting with pride.

When the show was over Mrs Pepperpot looked at the frog very pleadingly and said: 'Don't you think you could just show me how you dive? I *would* like to try that.'

'Well,' he said, 'you won't find it very easy to begin with, but it would do no harm to try at this end, I suppose. I'll give you a demonstration first.' And with that he made a perfect dive off the little rock.

When he came up again he told Mrs Pepperpot to point her arms straight up and to let herself go forwards till they were pointing down into the water.

'Shut your eyes as you go in,' he warned.

Mrs Pepperpot stood on the edge of the rock.

'It looks a bit deep,' she said. She was feeling rather frightened.

'It has to be,' said the frog, 'or you'd knock your head on the bottom. Off you go now; I'll be here to save you!'

So Mrs Pepperpot pointed her arms in the air, held her breath, shut her eyes and let herself fall forward. But instead of the beautiful dive she had hoped to make right under the water and up again, she found herself rolling about in what seemed more like a large puddle than a deep pool; she had GROWN!

As she picked herself up and waded out of the water

to the bank she could see no sign of the frog or the tadpoles. Her clothes were clinging to her, and though she tried to dry her arms and legs, it was no use putting on her shoes and stockings, so she hurried home in her bare feet, leaving a great dripping trail behind her.

As soon as she got home she remembered what her husband had said: 'You'll catch your death of cold!' So she changed into dry clothes and hid the wet ones in the attic. Then she quickly set about making her husband's favourite macaroni pie for supper.

It was several days before Mrs Pepperpot got a chance to go back to the pool. But all the time she was longing to find out if she had really learned to swim. So, when she heard the children going home through the wood one warm evening, she slipped out of the house and made for the pool as fast as she could go. She looked pretty queer, because this time she was wearing an old long bathing suit of her husband's she had found in the attic, and over it she had her winter coat. She just hoped that no one would see her.

When she got to the pool all was quiet. She didn't dare to dive in, but from the big rock she let herself slide into the water, and before she knew it, there she was, swimming along – not quite as stylishly as the frog, rather more like a dog paddling – but still, she was swimming and Mrs Pepperpot felt very proud.

As she turned to swim back to the rock she noticed she was being followed. There was the frog keeping pace with her, and behind him were all the tadpoles, in close formation, from the largest to the tiniest, no bigger than a lady-bird! For one moment the frog came to the top of the water and gave a loud croak.

'Thanks, Mr Frog,' said Mrs Pepperpot, 'you're the best swimming teacher in the world!'

With an elegant kick of his back legs, the frog did a nose-dive down into the dark depths of the pool, and all the tadpoles followed after and Mrs Pepperpot couldn't see them any more.

So now you know how Mrs Pepperpot learned to swim.

Mrs Pepperpot
Gives a Party

M rs Pepperpot likes animals, as you know, but until lately Mr Pepperpot wasn't so keen; in fact, he didn't like *baby* animals at all.

'Messy things,' he used to say, 'always getting in the way and making too much noise!'

'It's all very well for you,' said Mrs Pepperpot, 'out seeing people all day long. But I'm here all alone, and I like to have little creatures round me for company.'

There was no answer to that, so Mr Pepperpot

would go off to work muttering: 'Just keep them out of my way, that's all!'

One day when a stray kitten came to the door mewing to come in, Mrs Pepperpot picked it up and brought it indoors. Then she found it had lost a bit of its tail, and though it was mending, it was still very sore.

'Oh, you poor stumpy wee thing!' said Mrs Pepperpot, stroking the kitten, which was trembling with cold and hunger. 'I'll put you in the box under the stove where it's nice and warm, and you shall have some bread and milk.'

Soon the kitten was sleeping contentedly in the box and was so quiet that Mr Pepperpot never noticed it was there when he came home from work.

A few days later, when Mrs Pepperpot was bringing her shopping home from the village, she came past Mr Hog's pig-sty, where the sow had had twelve piglets. She stopped to watch them scampering round, and then she noticed that one of them was limping. It was the smallest of the litter and all the other piglets were pushing it about, so that it couldn't even get to its mother to suckle.

'You're having a pretty thin time, Squiggly,' said Mrs Pepperpot, as she leaned over the fence and picked up the piglet, which was now squealing loudly. Just then the farmer came out to feed the sow, and Mrs Pepperpot held up the piglet to show him.

'Look, Mr Hog, this piglet has broken its leg!'

'So it has!' said Mr Hog. 'Well, we'll have to have roast suckling pig for dinner this Sunday.'

He reached out to take the animal from her, but Mrs Pepperpot said: 'Oh no, that would be a shame!' and hung on to the piglet which was quietly grunting by now.

'What else can I do? The others will kill it if I leave it in the sty,' said Mr Hog.

'I'll buy it from you and rear it by hand,' said Mrs Pepperpot, though she wondered how she was going to pay for it.

'I'll give it to you and welcome, Mrs Pepperpot, if you think you can do anything with it,' said Mr Hog.

So Mrs Pepperpot thanked him and went home with the piglet in her arms. When she got there she fixed a little wooden splint on the piglet's broken leg, gave him a good feed of milk and gruel and tucked him up in the box under the stove together with the kitten.

When Mr Pepperpot came home he was a bit startled to hear grunts from under the stove, but Mrs Pepperpot quickly explained that the piglet was a present from Mr Hog.

'It won't cost much to rear,' she said; 'we have plenty of potato peelings and scraps, and then when it's big enough we can sell it.'

This idea appealed to Mr Pepperpot, who liked to make a bit of extra money, so he didn't grumble any more.

Stumpy, the kitten, and Squiggly, the piglet, got on

very well together, and Mrs Pepperpot had a lot of fun watching them.

'Good things always come in threes,' she said to herself; 'I wonder what my third pet will be?'

She didn't have long to wait, because the next time she was down at the village store there was a man in there with a sack on his back. She could see there was something moving in the sack, so when they got outside she couldn't help asking what it was.

'Oh, it's just a puppy I'm going to drown,' said the man, who had a nasty leer on his face.

'A puppy?' exclaimed Mrs Pepperpot. 'What's the poor little thing done that you have to drown it?'

'He was the ugliest of the litter,' said the man, 'and as he's not pure-bred anyway, nobody wanted him.'

'Not pure-bred, eh?' Mrs Pepperpot was getting angry. 'Ugly, is he? Well, you wouldn't win much of a prize at a beauty-show yourself, mister! If you don't want the puppy you can give him to me; I'll see he gets a good home.'

'All right, all right, keep your hair on!' said the man, undoing the sack and lifting out a small black and white puppy with a pug-nose and a patch over one eye. 'He's all yours, free and for nothing!'

He handed the puppy to Mrs Pepperpot and walked off quickly before she could change her mind.

Mrs Pepperpot held the whimpering, frightened little puppy and stroked him: 'Well, Ugly, I don't know what Mr Pepperpot's going to say to another baby in the house, but I couldn't let you be drowned, could I?'

When she got home she put him in with the other two, and he wagged his little tail and made friends with the kitten and the piglet with no trouble at all. Mrs Pepperpot decided to tell her husband she was only keeping the puppy till she could find a home for it, but she didn't have to worry, for Mr Pepperpot never noticed the new addition to the family when he got back from work.

He sat down at the table and his eyes had a far-away look as he said: 'D'you know, wife? I've been thinking.'

'What have you been thinking?' asked his wife.

'There's one thing I've never been and I'd really like to be,' said Mr Pepperpot.

'Whatever can that be?' she wondered, thinking of all sorts of things Mr Pepperpot had never been.

'President of a club or society,' he said.

'Well!' said Mrs Pepperpot, she hadn't expected him to say that. 'Which club or society were you thinking of?'

'I don't know, but Eddie East told me the Sports Club is looking for a new president, and old Hatchet, the president of the Savings Club, died just last week, and then there's the Egg Co-operative Society . . .'

Mrs Pepperpot thought a bit, then she said: 'The best thing would be to give a party.'

'How d'you mean, give a party?' said Mr Pepperpot, who never liked to ask people to the house in case Mrs Pepperpot did her shrinking act.

'Oh, I don't mean a *big* party, just to ask the Easts

and the Wests – he's secretary in the Savings Club, you know – in for coffee and cakes one evening. Then, let me see, who's in the Egg Co-operative? Oh yes, that's Sarah South's husband, so we'll ask them too. What about next Saturday?'

Mrs Pepperpot was getting quite excited at the idea of giving a party, but her husband looked very doubtful. He shook his head: 'Not unless you promise not to shrink,' he said.

'Don't be silly,' said Mrs Pepperpot, 'you know I can't do that. But I *will* promise to get out of the way if I do shrink.'

'That's all very well,' said Mr Pepperpot, 'but how shall I know where you are?'

'When you hear a mouse squeak three times, you'll know it's me,' said Mrs Pepperpot, and when her husband still looked worried, she handed him a big plate of his favourite macaroni pie.

'Don't you fret,' she said, 'it'll be all right. Goodness! I've just remembered; if we ask the Easts and the Wests and the Souths, we shall *have* to ask the Norths as well.'

'Why? Ned North isn't in any society that I know of,' grumbled Mr Pepperpot. He wished now that he had never started the idea.

'All the same, we've been to their house, and this is a good way to ask them back. Let me see, that'll be eight guests: I shall have to make two layer cakes and lots of little sandwiches.'

'One thing I do know,' said Mr Pepperpot, 'all those

stray animals of yours will have to go out in the shed that night.'

'Certainly not!' cried his wife. 'They'd catch their death of cold! They're very well-behaved and will stay right where they are – under the kitchen stove!'

So the day was fixed and the guests all said they would come.

Mrs Pepperpot spent the whole day cleaning the house and baking layer cakes and making sandwiches. Then she put on her Sunday best and stood at the door to welcome her guests and everyone shook hands.

'Now do sit down and make yourselves at home,' said Mrs Pepperpot, bustling about. To her husband, who was standing in a corner looking helpless, she said: 'You'll keep everyone happy, won't you, dear, while I go out and heat the coffee?' And then she disappeared out into the kitchen.

Poor Mr Pepperpot! He was so unused to company that he didn't know where to begin, but just stood there shuffling his feet and scratching his head until, luckily, Mr East asked him a question.

'Are you going in for the ski-ing competition this year?' he asked.

'Well, I might,' said Mr Pepperpot, easing himself into a chair next to Mr East. 'I used to be pretty good when I was young, but of course I'm out of training now.'

'Oh, it wouldn't take you long to get back into form!' Mr East assured him and Mr Pepperpot forgot his shyness and was soon talking away about the races he had won and the spills he had had while all the rest of the party listened. It wasn't until he couldn't think of anything more to tell that he noticed his wife hadn't come back from the kitchen.

'Excuse me a moment,' he said, and rushed out, fearing the worst had happened. But there stood Mrs Pepperpot, as large as life, putting the finishing touches to the layer cakes.

'What's the matter?' she asked.

'Thank goodness you're still here!' said Mr Pepperpot.

'Of course I am! Everything's ready now, so hold the door open for me while I carry in the tray.'

They could hear the guests laughing in the living-room, and when they went in they found the piglet had sneaked in and was trying to run round the table.

'Did you ever see a sillier-looking piglet with a wooden splint on?' said Mrs Pepperpot, picking him up. 'I call him Squiggly, but my husband is so fond of pigs he wouldn't even let me get rid of the thing.'

Mr Pepperpot was so surprised to hear his wife say this that he took the pig from her and stroked it, muttering, 'Oh yes, I *love* piglets.' Then he handed it to Mrs North who wanted to hold it on her knee.

All went well while they sat at the table; everyone enjoyed the coffee and the delicious sandwiches and layer cake. As they chatted Mrs Pepperpot cleverly brought the conversation round to savings. She told Mr West: 'My husband is such a good manager; he always knows exactly what money we have to spend on what!' Which was true enough, for he usually just said 'no' whenever she asked for money to spend on anything except food.

Mr West said, 'Is that so?' and started asking Mr Pepperpot some questions. Soon they were talking about all sorts of money matters, so Mr Pepperpot didn't notice his wife leaving the room again. When he looked up and found her gone he quickly excused himself to go and look for her.

She was not in the kitchen!

Frantically he called: 'Wife! Where are you?'

'Here I am!' she answered, as calmly as you please. She had been to the bedroom to fetch a pillow for Mrs East's back.

'Oh dear, I don't know where I am when you keep disappearing like this!' said Mr Pepperpot.

'I wish you'd stop fussing and just look after our guests,' Mrs Pepperpot said.

Just then they heard a great noise of laughter and squeaks and yaps, and when they opened the door to the living-room there were Mr North and Mr East on their hands and knees on the floor, while Squiggly the pig and Ugly the pup were chasing each other round and round the two men. Everyone else was laughing and clapping and egging them on.

'You certainly know how to amuse your guests!' said Mr West, who was too fat to join in the fun on the floor.

'My husband just loves to have animals around,' said Mrs Pepperpot. 'I never know what he's going to bring home next.' She gave her husband a great nudge to make him say something nice, but Mr Pepperpot was so overcome by all the things that were happening he just said, 'Mm, ah!' and shooed the pup and the piglet back into the kitchen.

Now Mrs Pepperpot thought it was time they talked about hens, as her husband had said that he might like to be president of the Egg Co-operative Society. So she told the guests how well he looked after their hens and what wonderful eggs they produced. She even told them how he always knew what to do if one of the hens became ill.

Her husband listened in astonishment as he knew very well that it was Mrs Pepperpot who looked after the hens and he hardly ever saw them, but he couldn't stop her now, so he just let her talk till the guests got up and said it was time to go home.

'We've had such a nice evening,' said Norah North as they shook hands at the door, and all the others said much the same, while Mr Pepperpot held a torch for them to see their way down the path.

After they were all safely away he came indoors. Taking out his spotted handkerchief, he wiped his face and said: 'Am I glad that's over! All the same I don't really think they'll make me president of any of their societies.'

A squeaky little voice answered: 'You wait and see!'

Startled, Mr Pepperpot looked round: 'Who said that?' he asked.

'Peep, peep, peep!' said the little voice, and then he

remembered that this was the signal his wife was to give him if she had turned small.

'Where are you hiding now?' he asked, but she wanted to tease him, so she let him search all through the house before she told him.

'Here I am!' she called at last from a drawer under the kitchen stove. 'I've decided to sleep with *your* pets tonight!'

'My pets!' he snorted. 'What's come over you? I never heard you tell so many fibs in all the years we've been married.'

'I was only trying to help,' said Mrs Pepperpot in her tiny voice, 'and, as a matter of fact, I think I managed it rather well! As they were going down the path I heard Ned North say to his wife that he thought you'd be the right person to be President of the Society for the Protection of Helpless Animals.'

'Well, I'll be blowed!' said Mr Pepperpot.

'I hope you're pleased,' said Mrs Pepperpot. 'I did my best. And now I think I'll say good night!' and she snuggled down with Stumpy, the kitten, Squiggly, the piglet and Ugly, the pup.

As for Mr Pepperpot, well, he'd got his wish; they really did ask him to be president of the Society for the Protection of Helpless Animals, and from then on he had to be kind to *all* animals, whether he liked them or not.

Sir Mark the Valiant

There was once a little boy called Mark who had to stay in bed because he had whooping cough. His friends couldn't visit him in case they too caught the whooping cough, but he didn't really mind, as he had something very special to play with.

That something special was a castle which stood on a little table by Mark's bed. It had a tower and ramparts and a moat with a drawbridge over it, and it was made to look as if it had been built long, long ago. Actually, it was made in a modern factory, and Mark's father had bought it cheaply in a sale. But Mark hated to hear his mother tell people it was cheap; he thought it was so grand and beautiful, it ought to have cost lots and lots of money.

Mark also had a flag which he put on the tower and a handsome knight, dressed in white armour and riding on a white horse with a long mane and tail. The knight he called Sir Guy and he put him on the ramparts to keep a watch for enemies. The horse had its head turned a little, as if it was looking for enemies to come and attack the castle from behind.

There were many windows in the castle; in the tower, which had a winding staircase, there were narrow slits and in the top of the tower there was just one window with bars.

'That is where Sir Guy puts his prisoners,' Mark told his mother.

The little boy played with the castle all day long, and at night when his mother put it back on the table, he would lie gazing at it till he fell asleep. Sometimes the coughing would be so bad that it made his eyes water so that he saw everything through a haze; then the castle seemed to be shimmering with lights from every window – except one; the barred window in the tower was always dark.

'Sir Guy will put the light on when he puts his prisoner there,' said Mark.

One night he had been coughing and whooping so much that both his father and mother had sat with him, one holding his poor head and the other his hand.

At last it stopped and he could breathe more comfortably. So his mother gave him some medicine and his father tucked him up, and then they both said good night and put out the light.

Mark was very tired; he lay there rubbing his eyes and then he looked at the castle. It looked so beautiful with the lights shimmering in every window – *every* window? Mark sat up in bed; even the barred window in the tower was lit up tonight! And what was that? Surely Sir Guy was moving? Yes, his head was moving from side to side, and now he was lifting his hand to shade his eyes, as if he was searching for something in the distance. Now the horse moved its head too and pawed the ground with its right foreleg!

Suddenly Sir Guy dug his spurs in, galloped over the drawbridge and headed his horse straight up the counterpane towards Mark's chest! It looked as if he were riding through a flowery meadow and the horse's mane and tail were flying in the wind!

Just before they reached Mark's chin, the knight reined in his horse so that it reared on its hind legs.

'To battle! To battle!' shouted Sir Guy, drawing his sword and waving it over his head. 'Rally to me, my men!' The horse neighed loudly, reared again and waved its hooves so near to Mark's face, he thought he was going to kick him. But he lay quite still, as he didn't want to frighten them away.

'Where are my men?' shouted Sir Guy. 'They have deserted me in my hour of need! Who will follow me now?' he said, and then he pointed his sword at Mark; 'Will you be my squire and fight by my side?'

'I'd like to,' said Mark, 'but who's the enemy?'

'Haven't you heard?' said the knight. 'Didn't you see the light in the prison window? I'm getting ready to capture Sir Hugh. Then I will lock him up in the tower for the rest of his life.'

'How will you find him?' asked Mark.

'A message came to me that he is on his way. But now, alas, my men have fled and I have no one to help me except you.'

'I will do my best,' Mark promised, 'but who is Sir Hugh?'

'He is the most fearsome knight in the whole land; wherever he goes he leaves terror behind, castles burned and people robbed and killed. No one has ever defeated him in battle and it is known that he is afraid of only one thing.'

'What is that?' asked Mark.

'Ah!' cried the knight. 'If we knew that the task would be easy! But he keeps the secret well and no one knows what it is he fears!'

'Oh well,' said Mark, 'he'll have to be pretty big to frighten me!'

At that moment he heard a hollow laugh which seemed to be coming from behind the medicine bottle on the table beside his bed.

'So you're not afraid of me, eh?' It sounded more like a snarl than a voice, and before Mark could answer, a knight in shining red armour from head to foot rushed forward to the edge of the table and took a flying leap right on to the bed! Sir Guy moved a little nearer to Mark's chin.

'I heard you were looking for me, Sir Guy!' shouted Sir Hugh, waving his sword over his head. 'Well, here I am and I challenge you to battle on this plain!' And he pointed to the part of the counterpane that covered Mark's tummy.

Sir Guy had now gathered up his courage; he jumped off his horse, which trotted behind him, and he ran full tilt down Mark's chest, shouting: 'Have at you, Sir Hugh, in the King's name!'

The two knights came together in a great clash of swords. They hit each other on their helmets, breastplates and shields. Back and forth they went, and Mark watched spellbound to see which one would go down first.

Suddenly Sir Hugh's sword knocked Sir Guy down and Sir Hugh picked him up and tucked him under one arm and his horse under the other.

'Ah ha!' shouted Sir Hugh. 'I have you at my mercy!' Then he turned to Mark and shouted at him, 'I challenge you, Moonface, to come to his aid!'

Just then Mark started coughing. He whooped and he whooped and the whole bed shook like an earthquake. Sir Hugh dropped Sir Guy and his horse and they all ran this way and that, trying to find a place where the ground wasn't heaving under them!

When at last Mark stopped and everything became

quiet once more, he saw both the knights pick themselves up and walk towards his face. Sir Hugh was in front and came as close as he dared. Then he said: 'Tell me, Moonface, what caused the earth to tremble? Are you a magician?'

'Oh no, sir,' answered Mark, 'I just have the whooping cough.'

Sir Hugh looked at him with horror in his eyes: 'Did you say whooping cough?'

'That's right,' said Mark, 'I've had it for a week now.'

'Who told you of my one fear in life?' thundered Sir Hugh, shaking his fists at Mark, his face almost as red as his armour.

'No one, sir,' said Mark, 'but it's a very catching illness and I'm afraid the germs will attack you any minute now.'

'Oh no!' shouted Sir Hugh as he ran full tilt to the bottom end of the bed. 'Let me get away from here!'

'If I were you, sir,' said Mark, 'I would lock myself up in a room until the danger of infection is over.'

'I will, I will!' cried Sir Hugh, whose knees were knocking inside his armour by now, he was so frightened. 'But where can I go?'

'Well,' said Mark, 'I suggest you walk across that drawbridge, open the door at the bottom of the tower, climb the winding staircase until you reach the top. There you will find a little room with bars across the window, and if you lock the door you will be quite safe.'

Before you could say knife, that knight was scurrying across the drawbridge and disappearing through the door into the tower! A moment later Mark could see his face peering through the bars of the lighted prison window!

'Hurrah!' shouted Sir Guy, who had been standing near Mark's face, watching. 'That was a master stroke! You have defeated the King's worst enemy, and for this good deed His Majesty will justly reward you!' Facing Mark and raising his sword in his right hand, Sir Guy then said: 'From the bottom of my heart I thank you and salute you, Sir Mark the Valiant!'

'It's very kind of you, sir,' said Mark, 'but I only told him about my whooping cough.'

But Sir Guy paid no attention. He was striding across the counterpane to where his horse stood. The horse whinnied as the knight swung himself into the saddle, and then it trotted quietly towards the drawbridge. Soon the knight was back in his place on the ramparts, looking into the distance in front of him, while his horse turned its head to see if there were enemies coming up from behind.

In the morning Mark woke up feeling better. What a strange dream he had had! He looked at the castle to see if he could see Sir Hugh peering through the bars of the lighted prison window. There on one side stood the white horse with Sir Guy on its back, just as he had left it the night before. But there was no light in any of the windows.

Mark's mother came in at that moment with his breakfast.

'Good morning, Mark!' she said, and then she looked at him more closely. 'You look *much* better today,' she said, 'the whooping cough must be nearly over.'

'Yes,' said Mark, 'we had a battle last night and I won! I am now Sir Mark the Valiant and my castle is called "Castle Valiant".'

His mother smiled and said he must have been dreaming, but Mark thought it was all too real to have been a dream.

Mrs Pepperpot
Turns Detective

Mrs Pepperpot has tried her hand at many jobs, but this autumn she has tried something new – she has turned detective.

Of all the seasons Mrs Pepperpot likes autumn best. When anyone complains that it's dark and dreary, she always answers that it's the best time of the year, because then we get the reward for all the hard work we put in in the spring with our digging and sowing and planting.

'But the days get so short and the nights get so long!' they say.

'That makes it all the cosier indoors,' says Mrs Pepperpot, 'and think of all the fun the children have, playing detectives with torches in the dark.'

'All right, but what about the burglars and suchlike? They have a much better chance to do their stealing at this time of year.'

So the argument ran, but Mrs Pepperpot said no more, because you see, someone had been stealing from *her*, and she very much wanted to play detective herself.

And what d'you think was being stolen from Mrs Pepperpot? Her potatoes, of all things! Ever since September, when she first started digging them up, she had been finding plants with no potatoes under them; they had been dug up, the potatoes taken off and then the plants stuck back in the soil to make them look as if they were still growing. Wasn't that a cunning trick?

Mrs Pepperpot couldn't think who it could be. If only she were a *real* detective, then she could trace footprints in the mud, perhaps even fingerprints on the leaves of the potato-plants. She could build a secret observation post and carry a gun, and when she had caught the thief red-handed, she would say: 'Hands up!'

At supper one night she was thinking so hard about being a detective that she said 'Hands up!' when she was passing a bowl of hot stew to her husband, and he

71

dropped it all over the clean table-cloth in his fright. For once she couldn't very well scold him.

After supper she remembered she had left her potato bucket out in the field almost full of potatoes. 'I'd better fetch it in, or the thief might take that too,' she thought.

She put a scarf round her head and found the torch, for it was a very dark night. Then she went out to the field and was just bending down to pick up the bucket when she heard someone climbing through the hedge. Quickly she put out the torch and got right down on her knees over the bucket, so that she couldn't be seen.

'I'll catch him this time!' she said to herself and her heart was going pitterpat with excitement! But was she *cross* a moment later, when she found herself sprawling among the potatoes in the bucket; she had SHRUNK, of course.

It wasn't even any good trying to climb out of the bucket; because how could she get through all that mud back to the house while she was tiny? And she did so want to catch the thief! So, there was nothing for it but to lie where she was and try and see what the thief looked like.

First she listened very carefully; there was someone climbing through the hedge, right enough. But what was that? Two more people seemed to be coming through, and they were not being very quiet about it, either! Now she could hear them whispering to each other: 'Mind how you go!' This was a *boy's* voice.

'I had to pull him through the hedge!' answered a *girl's* voice.

'She hurt me!' wailed another younger voice.

'Ssh!' whispered the big boy, 'or we'll go straight home and not get any potatoes tonight!'

Mrs Pepperpot could hear them coming down one of the rows with a spade. They also had a bucket which rattled. The steps stopped. Now she could hear the spade going into the soil.

'Look, Sis,' said the big boy's voice, 'these are wopping great potatoes. Hold the bucket!'

The smaller child's footsteps started coming in Mrs Pepperpot's direction and in another moment he had found her bucket.

'Tum here, tum here!' he called in a high baby voice, quite forgetting he had promised to keep quiet.

'What is it?' hissed the big boy. 'Don't shout!' But the little boy went on: 'Lots o' 'tatoes in a bucket!' he announced.

'I'll give you lots o' 'tatoes in a bucket!' muttered Mrs Pepperpot to herself; 'I'll have you all three arrested when I get back to my proper size.'

Then, as quietly as she could, she worked her way down under the top layer of potatoes, so that the children wouldn't see her. It was only just in time, as the big boy and the girl came over to have a look, and they were so pleased with little brother's find that the big boy lifted up the bucket and made for the hedge.

'You carry the other bucket,' whispered the big boy to the little one, 'it's not so heavy.'

73

'I dood! I dood!' piped the little fellow who couldn't say his 'k's' and 'g's'. 'I find lots o' 'tatoes!' and he scrambled after the others, dragging the lighter bucket after him.

'It's a good thing it's so dark,' said the big boy, as they all got through the hedge on to the path, 'no one can see us here.'

The girl shivered a little: 'I feel like a real burglar in a detective story,' she said.

'I burgle-burgle,' chimed in the little one.

'Burglars don't usually carry detectives around in buckets!' said Mrs Pepperpot to herself. 'Just you wait, my fine friends!'

At last the children stopped at a door. They knocked and called: 'Open the door, Mother, and see what we've brought!'

The door opened and Mrs Pepperpot heard a woman's voice say: 'My! That's a fine bucketful; it'll keep us well fed for days. I'll heat the water in the pot straight away.'

'I ha' some too!' shouted the youngest, showing her the big potatoes in his bucket.

'Two buckets! That means you've taken one that doesn't belong to us. One of you'll have to take it back when you've eaten.'

'But, Mother!' said the boy.

'There's no "but" about it,' said his mother firmly. 'We may be so poor we have to help ourselves to a few potatoes now and then, but I hope to make it up to the owner of that field before too long. The bucket goes straight back!'

Mrs Pepperpot could hardly believe her ears; here was a family right on her door-step, so to speak, and she didn't know they were going hungry. They must be new to the neighbourhood, or surely someone would have helped them. Well, she would certainly let them have whatever potatoes they needed, no doubt about that. She had almost forgotten she was being a detective and a doll's size one at that, when the mother started lifting the potatoes out of the bucket to put them in the saucepan, which was now bubbling on the stove.

Poor Mrs Pepperpot! What should she do?

'A fine thing!' she said to herself, burrowing deeper and deeper into the bucket to hide herself. 'Here I am, being sorry for them because they're poor, when I ought to be sorry for myself, going to be boiled alive any minute now!'

At last all the potatoes were in the pot and only Mrs Pepperpot was left, but by now she was so covered in earth that the mother didn't notice her.

But the little boy did. He was peering into the bucket, and he put his small hand in and lifted Mrs Pepperpot out.

'That's torn it!' said Mrs Pepperpot and shut her eyes.

'What a funny li'l 'tato!' said the little boy. 'I teep it.' And he ran off with her into the scullery, where he hid behind the door. The rest of the family were too taken up with getting the meal ready to notice where he went.

Sitting on a box, the little boy held Mrs Pepperpot very carefully on his knee.

'You my 'tato?' he asked.

Mrs Pepperpot nodded: 'That's right. I'm your 'tato.'

The little boy's eyes grew round with amazement. 'You *talking* 'tato?' he asked.

'That's right,' said Mrs Pepperpot again. 'I'm a talking 'tato.'

'Tan I eat you?' he asked, looking at her very closely.

Mrs Pepperpot shivered a bit, but she spoke very calmly: 'I don't think I would, if I were you, sonny. I don't make very good eating.'

Just then his mother called him to eat his dinner. So he put Mrs Pepperpot down on the box and said: 'I ha' dinner now. You my talking 'tato – you stay here – I tum back soon play wi' you.'

'Well, sonny,' said Mrs Pepperpot, 'I may have to go, but I'll come back tomorrow and then I'll bring you a present. How's that?'

'You bring me 'nother talking 'tato!' he said and ran back to his mother who was putting a great heap of mashed potato on his plate.

Mrs Pepperpot wondered what she should do next. If she climbed back into the bucket and waited for a ride home in that, it might take hours before the boy went back to the field, and Mr Pepperpot would be fretting about her. Just then there was a little scratching noise behind the box and a mouse peeped out.

'Hullo,' said Mrs Pepperpot in mouse-language.

The mouse came out to look at her, and Mrs Pepperpot had never seen such a skinny creature.

'If you'll help me get out of here,' she said, 'I have a nice piece of bacon at home you can have.'

The mouse pricked up its ears. 'Bacon, did you say? We haven't seen bacon in this house for a very long time.'

'Why d'you stay here if there's so little to eat?' asked Mrs Pepperpot, as she got on the mouse's back.

'Well,' said the mouse, starting off through a hole in the wall, 'I've been with the family all my life, you know, so I don't like to leave them in the lurch. I mean, what would people say if they found out there wasn't enough food here to feed a mouse?'

When they got to the foot of the hill leading to her house, Mrs Pepperpot thanked the mouse and promised to put the piece of bacon behind the box in the scullery the next day. Then she very conveniently grew large and hurried on home.

Mr Pepperpot was standing at the front door, anxiously peering out into the dark. 'Where have you been all this time?' he asked.

'Looking for my bucket of potatoes,' said Mrs Pepperpot. 'Can't you see how grubby I am? Crawling on my hands and knees in the mud I was, but I couldn't find it anywhere.'

Did the boy bring back the bucket? Did Mrs Pepperpot

have the children arrested? And what about the little boy's talking 'tato? Well, all that is part of another story.

Mrs Pepperpot
and the Brooch Hunt

The last time Mrs Pepperpot tried her hand at playing detective you may remember she nearly ended up as mashed potato. But she still has a secret longing to be one of those smart detectives you see on the films – the kind that solve everything as easy as winking.

Meanwhile, she has decided not to arrest those potato thieves. Instead, she goes to see the family almost every day and she knows all their names. There's Mrs Grey, the mother, who tries to keep the home together. It's very difficult for her, because her husband's been out of work for many months and now he's gone to the coast to see if he can get a job on a boat. Then there's Peter, who is ten and a sensible boy, and Betty, who is eight, and little Bobby, who is only three. He keeps asking about his talking potato, and, though the other children don't know what he's talking about, Mrs Pepperpot does, so she has bought him a clockwork frog to play with instead.

Each time she visits the Greys she brings some potatoes, and she doesn't forget the hungry mouse, either; he gets a bit of bacon rind behind the door in the scullery. When she goes home the children often walk part of the way with her and talk about all sorts of things.

Once she happened to say that she had lost a little silver brooch – one she had been given as a christening present.

'I hate to lose it,' she told the children, 'because I've had it all my life and it's a pretty little thing.'

'Why don't you let us be detectives and help you find it?' Peter asked.

'Oh yes!' cried Betty, clapping her hands. 'That would be fun!'

'*I* want to be deti–deti too!' shouted Bobby, dancing up and down.

'Oh, it's hardly worth making too much fuss about,' said Mrs Pepperpot, though she secretly rather liked the idea.

'Come on, Mrs Pepperpot,' said Peter, putting on a grown-up detective sort of voice, 'tell us where you last remember seeing the lost item.'

Mrs Pepperpot smiled: 'Now, let me see; I think I wore it at Nelly North's when we had a club meeting there last month.'

Peter got out a piece of paper and pencil and noted this down.

'Right,' he said, 'when can we start investigations?'

'Well,' said Mrs Pepperpot, 'I'm busy all day tomorrow with the washing, but we could meet here about four o'clock, and by then I may have thought where else I might have left it.'

'And we can work out a plan of campaign,' said Peter importantly.

So the children promised to meet Mrs Pepperpot by a certain big fir-tree on the road between their house and hers at four o'clock the next day, and they were very excited about it, especially little Bobby, who kept talking about the deti-detis till his mother put him to bed.

Next day at four o'clock sharp they all met at the tree. Mrs Pepperpot had brought a torch, because it got dark so early.

'First we'll walk over the meadow to Nelly North's Farm,' she said. 'I have an idea it might be under her sofa. She's not a very tidy person, but I don't want to offend her by hinting she hasn't cleaned her room properly, so I want you, Peter, to take this torch and shine it under the sofa while I keep Nelly talking. You must do it secretly, mind, so that she doesn't notice.'

'What about Bobby and me?' asked Betty.

'You'll have to keep watch outside,' said Mrs Pepperpot.

So they started off across the meadow, walking in single file along a narrow path with Mrs Pepperpot in front, shining the torch. Suddenly the torch flew up in the air and Mrs Pepperpot disappeared! At least, that's what the children thought, for, of course, *we* know that she had shrunk again! The torch was still alight when it landed, but Mrs Pepperpot had rolled into the long grass, and it was Bobby who found her and picked her up by one leg!

'Here's my talking 'tato!' he shouted, dangling poor Mrs Pepperpot upside down.

'Put it down, Bobby,' said Betty, 'it might bite!'

'No!' insisted Bobby, who had now set Mrs Pepperpot on his hand. 'It's my talking 'tato!'

Mrs Pepperpot had now got her breath back, so she said as quietly as she could: 'That's right, children, Bobby *has* seen me like this before.'

'Why, it's Mrs Pepperpot!' cried Peter and Betty together. 'However did you get so small?'

'That will take too long to explain,' said Mrs Pepperpot, 'but it happens to me from time to time, and last time Bobby found me in the bottom of the potato bucket, so that's why he thinks I'm a talking potato.'

'Let *me* hold you,' said Betty. 'I'll be very careful.'

'Yes, I think I would feel a bit safer,' said Mrs Pepperpot, as Bobby was jogging her up and down in his excitement, making her quite giddy.

'What about our search? Will we have to call it off?' asked Peter.

Mrs Pepperpot didn't like to disappoint them, and she'd already thought up a new plan, but first she made them promise never to tell anybody about her turning small.

'You must hold up your right hands, as they do in the films, and swear you will never speak of this to a living soul.'

Peter and Betty held up their right hands and repeated Mrs Pepperpot's words, but little Bobby had to be told he would get a hard smack if he ever said he'd seen a talking potato!

'Now,' said Mrs Pepperpot, 'instead of me going in to talk to Nelly North, I want Peter to knock at the door. When Nelly opens it he must say that he's collecting for – let's see – a home for worn-out car tyres. If he says it quickly she won't notice, and then when she's gone to the kitchen to look for a penny, you just switch on the torch and shine it under the sofa in the front room, and if you see a shining object, bring it with you. Betty and Bobby and I will be waiting behind that tree over there.'

By now they had reached the road in front of North Farm and Mrs Pepperpot pointed her tiny hand at a tree standing a little way from the house.

'Right oh!' said Peter and walked bravely over to the door, hiding the torch in his pocket.

The others waited in the dark till he came back. It didn't take long, but Peter was quite excited when he came towards them, and he was holding something in his hand.

'Let me see!' said Mrs Pepperpot, who was standing on Betty's hand. Peter put the object down beside her and shone the torch on it.

'Oh dear!' she said. 'I'm afraid you've picked up the wrong thing. This is a silver ring that was sent to Nelly from her uncle in America; she said she had lost it the day of the meeting.'

Peter's face had fallen. 'What do we do now?'

'It's no good going back, you would find it too hard to explain,' said Mrs Pepperpot. 'Put it in your pocket while we go on to Sally South's house just along the road here. That's another place I think I may have dropped my brooch when I was there for the silver-wedding party.'

So they walked on to Sally South's house, Mrs Pepperpot riding in Betty's pocket and Bobby kept putting his fingers in to see if she was still there.

Sally didn't know Peter when she opened the door to him, and she was a bit deaf, so she didn't quite catch what he was collecting for, but he looked a nice boy, so she went off for a penny from her money-box. While she was out of the room Peter got the chance to shine his torch under the furniture and even behind the grandfather clock. There he saw something glittering, so he fished it out and put it in his pocket. When Sally came back he thanked her very nicely for the penny and ran back to the others who were hiding outside.

'Did you find it?' whispered Betty.

'I think so,' said Peter, bringing the little thing out of his pocket.

But when she saw it Mrs Pepperpot shook her head; 'Sorry, Peter, I'm afraid that's not it either. It's a medallion Sally's husband gave her for a silver-wedding present. He was very cross when he found she had dropped it that day.'

Peter looked quite disheartened. 'This doesn't seem such a good idea, after all,' he said. 'Perhaps we'd better give it up.'

'Is that the way for Detective Sergeant Peter Grey to speak?' demanded Mrs Pepperpot, who was really enjoying the hunt, though it was true she wasn't doing the hard work! 'Let's try East Farm; Mr Pepperpot and I were there just after Christmas for the baby's christening. I was godmother, so I carried the baby, and I expect the brooch fell off when I was putting the baby in his cot.'

'Can I carry my talking 'tato now?' asked Bobby who had been very good and quiet for a long time.

'All right, but don't you drop me now,' said Mrs Pepperpot, whose clothes and hair were getting quite messed up with all this passing from hand to hand.

When they got to East Farm only Mr East was at home, looking after the baby. He was a kindly man and never minded giving children the odd penny. So he put down his newspaper and went out to search for a coin in his jacket pocket. The baby was lying in a cot, playing with his toes. Peter remembered what Mrs Pepperpot had said about putting the baby in his cot, so when he saw a small silver bell in the cot beside the baby, he quickly picked it up and pocketed it. Mr East came in and gave him the penny, and Peter thanked him politely and ran out to the others.

'I hope I've got the right thing this time!' he cried, jingling the little bell as he pulled it out of his pocket.

'Oh, you silly boy!' exclaimed Mrs Pepperpot, 'how could you think that was my brooch? It belongs to the baby's rattle which I gave him myself for a christening present!'

Peter looked very sheepish; 'Well, you see, I don't really know what a brooch *is*!'

'Why didn't you say so before?' Mrs Pepperpot was beginning to get cross. 'A detective needs to know what he's looking for!'

'*I* know what a brooch is,' said Betty, 'it has a pin which fits into a clasp and you put it in your shawl.'

'That's right,' said Mrs Pepperpot who was trying hard to think where else they could search. 'I've got it. I'm sure I wore it for Paul West's confirmation. It was pouring with rain that day and I took my umbrella; I bet it dropped into the umbrella stand at West Farm. Come along, children, if it isn't there we'll go home, I promise you.'

So they turned about and trudged down a little lane till they got to West Farm. Peter knocked, as before, but this time there was no answer, so he tried the handle and the door opened. There, just inside, was the umbrella stand Mrs Pepperpot had told him about, so he quickly shone his torch right down to the bottom of it, and, Goodness Gracious! there he could see a small pin with what looked like the letter 'P' on it! Surely that must be it, thought Peter, and made a dive for it. Then he ran out to the others, hoping no one had heard him.

This time they were hiding behind a shed and Peter made sure he was out of sight of the house before he opened his hand: 'There,' he said, 'I've got it!'

'Show me,' said Mrs Pepperpot, but then she almost cried: 'This isn't my brooch – it's a tie-pin!'

'But it had "P" on it, so I thought it must be Pepperpot!' stammered poor Peter.

'I wasn't christened Pepperpot, was I? I only married him! The "P" stands for Paul who was confirmed that day. Goodness, how careless everybody is with their belongings!'

There was nothing for it now; they would have to give up and go home. What bothered Mrs Pepperpot was how to return all those things to their rightful owners. For once she really hadn't been very clever.

The three children were tired and walking slowly along the road, Betty holding Mrs Pepperpot, when suddenly they heard running footsteps coming in their direction.

'They're after us!' squeaked Mrs Pepperpot. 'Run, children!'

In their fright the children nearly fell over each other and poor Mrs Pepperpot was thrown right over the ditch into the field.

The footsteps were coming nearer.

'Stop, thief!' shouted someone. It was Nelly North. 'I can see them.'

'There's the boy!' shouted Sally South who was following her.

Mr East was plodding behind with fat Mrs West. 'Come on, boy,' he shouted, 'you might as well give up!'

The children were crying by now and little Bobby stumbled over a stone and fell.

At that moment a small, but commanding voice came through the air. 'Hands up or I shoot!' it shouted. It seemed to be coming from nowhere and everyone stood stock still. Then it spoke again: 'This is the secret police calling with a message for the following people: Mrs North, Mrs South, Mr East and Mrs West. Stand by, please! Can you hear me?'

They were all so surprised to hear their names called, that they very meekly answered, 'Yes'.

'Right,' went on the voice. 'You can all expect a surprise in your letter-boxes tomorrow morning. On one condition, that you immediately go home and leave the children alone!'

The children had stopped running too, and watched with amazement as, one by one, Nelly North, Sally South, Mr East and fat Mrs West all turned about and walked away without a single look behind them.

'Phew!' said a voice right beside the children. There stood Mrs Pepperpot, as large as life. She was holding a dock-leaf in her hand and it was curled in the shape of a large cone.

'What's that for?' asked little Bobby who had picked

himself up and was *very* pleased to see his friend Mrs Pepperpot again.

'The secret police always carry loudspeakers!' she answered, smiling at the children. Then they all went home to her house and had nice hot cocoa and pancakes.

Next morning when Nelly North looked in her letter-box she found the silver ring she had lost, Sally South found her silver medallion, Mr East found the silver bell from the baby's rattle and Mrs West found her son's tie-pin. They certainly were surprised!

But the one who was most surprised was Mrs Pepperpot. When she opened her letter-box she found a little parcel in it, and inside was her brooch. There was also a note from Peter, which said:

Dear Mrs Pepperpot,

After the clue you gave us last night, your detectives have been able to solve the mystery. We have put your potato-bucket back in its place in the potato-field. Thank you.

Yours truly,
Detective Sergeant P. Grey

'Of course!' said Mrs Pepperpot to herself, 'I was wearing the brooch on the night when the potato thieves came, and I must have dropped it in the bucket!'

AFTERWORD

Have *you* ever wondered what it would be like to shrink to the size of a pepperpot? *I* have, and I think that at some time in their lives most people have imagined being very small or very big, or wondered what it would be like to be invisible or to fly like a bird. There are times when we would all like to be different from everyone else. This element of change-magic – satisfying a dream that we all share – is one of the reasons why the stories about the remarkable Mrs Pepperpot have become such firm favourites with children all over the world.

Ever since storytelling began, people have been fascinated by tales of men and women who are very much smaller than everyone else. Fairy stories like 'Tom Thumb' and 'Hop o' My Thumb' – both about boys who are no bigger than their fathers' thumbs – have been known in various forms for hundreds of years in many different countries, and, in our own time, Mary Norton's stories about the Borrowers – the miniature people who live behind the skirting-boards and beneath the floorboards of our houses and who make use of the little things we lose – are loved by children today. Of course, Mrs Pepperpot is very different from both Tom Thumb and the Borrowers – she is a perfectly ordinary woman who just happens to shrink from time to time, for no apparent reason!

But Mrs Pepperpot's habit of shrinking unexpectedly isn't the only reason why we enjoy reading about her adventures. Above all, it is her determined, brave and practical approach to her predicament that makes the stories so memorable. She never complains when she suddenly finds herself the size of a pepperpot, even though it may happen at very awkward times – when she's just about to cut down a Christmas tree, for instance, or on the morning when she's planned to clean the house. 'Ah well, I could be in a worse fix, I suppose,' she says in the first story in this book. 'I ought to be used to it by now.' And she always knows how to put her small size to practical use.

Mind you, Mrs Pepperpot has her faults too. She has a peppery temper to match her name and she doesn't suffer fools gladly. She can be a little vain too: when she sees herself in a mirror, dressed as Sleeping Beauty, she has to admit that 'she looked rather wonderful'!

And it's not just Mrs Pepperpot who makes the stories so amusing. Her long-suffering husband is a wonderful character too. He is very patient with Mrs Pepperpot's strange behaviour but he receives little thanks for it. 'You silly man!' Mrs Pepperpot snaps at him when, in the first story, he thinks that he's lost her, and 'Eating! That's all you think of!' she says, when he complains that his supper isn't ready. In 'Mrs Pepperpot Learns to Swim', poor Mr Pepperpot has a very hard time of it indeed: his wife knocks his soup off the stove and he has to eat bread and dripping instead, then she knocks him out of bed and smacks him on the nose.

No wonder he goes to sleep on the kitchen floor! But, even though Mrs Pepperpot may snap at her husband sometimes, she is really very fond of him, and makes his favourite macaroni pie when she comes home from her swimming lesson with the frog. Indeed, Mrs Pepperpot always does her best to make sure that her surprising adventures do not interfere with her domestic duties: when the crows try to stop her going home, she remembers right away that the fishmonger is due to call on Wednesday and that she has to do the cleaning on Friday.

The setting of these stories adds to their charm, and we are always aware that they take place in Norway. The Magic Wood consists of larch and spruce and birch trees, and ogres and a polar bear appear in the stories. The special Scandanavian festivals play an important part too, especially in the story 'Midsummer Eve with the Ogres', which describes how Midsummer Eve is celebrated with bonfires and fireworks, and the houses are decorated with greenery and garlands of flowers. These traditional features of Norwegian life contrast with settings familiar to us all, like the television studio where Mrs Pepperpot has her adventure with the puppet-man. It is contrasts such as this which make the stories so intriguing – we see the ordinary and the fantastic side by side, and much of the appeal of Mrs Pepperpot herself rests on the fact that although extraordinary things do happen to her, she is really just an ordinary housewife.

Alf Prøysen was a master storyteller. Sadly, he died in

1970 and so there will be no new stories about Mrs Pepperpot. But there will always be new generations of children to discover this magical character for the first time, and those of us who know and love these enchanting stories can read them all over again, as often as we like.

Lance Salway

Some other Young Puffin Modern Classics

THE ADVENTURES OF THE LITTLE WOODEN HORSE
Ursula Moray Williams

CLEVER POLLY AND THE STUPID WOLF
Catherine Sefton

Some other Puffin Modern Classics

CARRIE'S WAR
Nina Bawden

CHARLOTTE'S WEB
E. B. White

THE CHILDREN OF GREEN KNOWE
Lucy Boston

THE DARK IS RISING
Susan Cooper

THE FRIENDS
Rosa Guy

THE MIDNIGHT FOX
Betsy Byars

MRS FRISBY AND THE RATS OF NIMH
Robert C. O'Brien

THE SILVER SWORD
Ian Serraillier

STIG OF THE DUMP
Clive King

THE TURBULENT TERM OF TYKE TYLER
Gene Kemp

Some other Young Puffin Modern Classics

ADVENTURES OF THE LITTLE WOODEN HORSE
Ursula Moray Williams

The Little Wooden Horse is Uncle Peder's finest creation, but when no one wants to buy him, he stays with his master and the two become great friends. When the toymaker grows poor and ill the brave little horse sets out to sell himself.

The Little Wooden Horse has adventures galore whilst trying to make enough money to return to his beloved master.

CLEVER POLLY AND THE STUPID WOLF
Catherine Storr

When Polly opens the door and finds a large black wolf standing on the doorstep waiting to gobble her up, it's the wolf that has the surprise when Polly invites him in.

Clever Polly isn't frightened at all and so begins a series of hilarious adventures as Polly tries to outwit the hungry but inexperienced wolf.

Some other Puffin Modern Classics

CARRIE'S WAR
Nina Bawden

Evacuated from London to Wales during the Second World War, Carrie and her brother are sent to live with the very strict Mr Evans.

But in trying to heal the breach between Mr Evans and his estranged sister, Carrie does the worst thing she ever did in her life.

CHARLOTTE'S WEB
E. B. White

This is the story of a little girl called Fern who loves a little pig called Wilbur. And of how Wilbur's dear friend Charlotte A. Cavatica, a beautiful grey spider, saves Wilbur from the usual fate of nice fat pigs, by a wonderfully clever plan (which no one else could possibly have thought of).

THE CHILDREN OF GREEN KNOWE
Lucy Boston

Tolly isn't looking forward to spending Christmas with his great-grandmother in her strange house, but as soon as he arrives at Green Knowe he is delighted by the very special kind of magic he finds all around him.

Indeed, far from being lonely, Tolly is caught up in a wonderful adventure with the other children who have lived there, eagerly learning all about the mysterious house and its delightful secrets.

THE DARK IS RISING
Susan Cooper

With only four days until Christmas, plenty of snow outside and his birthday to look forward to, Will has got everything in the world to feel happy about; but he has an overwhelming sense of foreboding.

Suddenly, as everyone else enjoys a normal Christmas, Will is caught up in a powerful and fantastic adventure, battling against the powers of Darkness and evil that threaten to destroy the world.

THE FRIENDS
Rosa Guy

Phyllisia is an outsider in a hostile new school. She's bullied and beaten up and she desperately needs a friend. But when Edith helps her, Phyllisia is not sure she wants to make friends with someone so scruffy.

It isn't until Phyllisia and Edith face real tragedy that they finally come to understand the value of true friendship.

THE MIDNIGHT FOX
Betsy Byars

Tom lives in the city and he is not looking forward to spending the summer holiday on his uncle's farm.

However, he learns to love the farm when he finds a black fox living in the woods. But his Uncle Fred wants to kill the fox and Tom is determined to help save her.

THE SILVER SWORD
Ian Serraillier

This is the story of four children's struggle to stay alive throughout the years of Nazi occupation and, afterwards, their epic journey from war-torn Poland to Switzerland in search of their parents.

Based on a true story, this is an extraordinarily moving account of life during and after the Second World War.

STIG OF THE DUMP
Clive King

One glorious day the ground gives way beneath Barney and he lands in a cave in the middle of the rubbish dump; and that's when he meets Stig.

Nobody believes his story, but for Barney Stig is totally real, and together they embark on a series of wonderful adventures.

DATE DUE

BRODART, CO.   Cat. No. 23-221